Two Crimson Smiles

by

TrishAnn Williams

Cover Art by *Lisa Dawn MacDonald*

The Wild Rose Press, Inc.
PO Box 708
Adams Basin, NY 14410-0708
Visit us at www.thewildrosepress.com

Publishing History
First Edition, 2024
Trade Paperback ISBN 978-1-5092-5481-1
Digital ISBN 978-1-5092-5482-8

Published in the United States of America

Dedication

To Barbara who left us too soon. Thanks for your
words of wisdom.

Prologue

"What has come from the earth goes back to the earth; so the cycle of life turns yet again."

A hush fell over the air–even the birds seemed to stop chirping as the group of pallbearers lowered the casket into the ground.

The woman in the black dress stood silently, watching as a scoop of rich soil cascaded over the mahogany casket. Imported lilies lined the pathway to the casket, and a soft string quartet played off to the side. No expense had been spared in the preparations for the funeral. Just as in life, death had come at great expense.

She was dressed elegantly in a designer black sheath dress. Her short black hair was slicked away from her face beneath a pillbox hat, revealing pale smooth skin – the delicate pallor broken only by an elegant slash of crimson lipstick. Her eyes were shielded by a short black veil. Her demeanor was understated, yet somehow formidable.

She stood alone facing the casket, with no one beside her to comfort her, yet she did not break down. She caught the pastor's eye, and he nodded at her. Taking a deep breath, the woman moved forward and placed a single rose on the casket.

Her final duty.

She looked up, past the rows of spectators who had come to pay their final respects. Past his family who had travelled in for the occasion. Past his colleagues who had spoken such generous words about him at the memorial service. Past the acquaintances quietly wiping tears with silk handkerchiefs.

Searching for the one person who knew the truth.

Dry-eyed, the woman did not turn back as she walked away from the gravesite. She made her way to the drive where two black Cadillacs waited, their engines nothing but a soft purr in the distance. As she placed her hand on the door of the first car, she heard the soft voice she had expected, yet dreaded at the same time.

"You didn't have to do that."

Steeling herself, the woman turned.

She stood face to face with another woman in a black dress. Her blond hair was tied loosely in a low ponytail. Her eyes were blue and clear, but heavy with sadness. Her lips, also red, didn't smile. She held, in her hands, a single rose.

How she didn't want to face this moment. To face this woman who was so entwined with her life. This woman she had never met before in her life.

She sighed and said in her soft, modulated voice, "I did. You deserve to be here. I know you loved him."

The other woman choked back a sob and then regained her composure, saying in a strangled voice, "We both loved him."

The woman smiled, a slash of crimson. "Yes, but only one of us killed him."

Chapter One

"You look lovely this evening."

Jane Rawlings smiled up at her husband as he placed a hand on her shoulder and squeezed. She kept her face impassive as a jolt seared her tender flesh where a deep bruise was covered by makeup.

Noticing his expectant stare, she hooked her arm through his and smiled. "Thank you. You look very handsome tonight as well," she echoed his words, gazing up at him with an admiring smile.

They made a stunning couple. A photo of them could cover the front page of any magazine. He was tall and dark, wearing an impeccably tailored suit and she was petite and trim, almost overwhelmed by the long black Dior dress she wore, but not quite.

Taking a deep breath, she adjusted the strap of the dress and followed her husband into the crowded ballroom of the largest hotel in Miami. Although just miles from the notorious nightlife Miami offered, this affair was formal and refined, a tribute to the old-fashioned money that Miami still boasted. The Grand Gala was the annual charity event for the Baptist Health South Florida hospital system, where her husband was a surgeon. As the name implied, everything about the event was luxurious and regal. Every bulb on the chandeliers twinkled in the dim ballroom and each flower arrangement was meticulously selected. A three-piece band played soft classical music that barely rose over the dim whispers of conversation floating through the air. Full bars stocked with liquors from around the world stood on each end of the massive room, which already brimmed with well-dressed society members and hospital staff. In the adjacent room, a silent auction represented the best of the best in everything the world offered. Jane knew her husband would bid on, and win, several self-indulgent items that neither of them needed or wanted.

As they moved through the room, Jane carried herself with a simple elegance that matched the designer dress. The diamonds on her ears and around her neck were of the highest quality, yet understated. The same words that could describe the woman wearing them.

Her husband gave her a quick glance. "I see Dr. Holding. Do you mind if I say hello?"

Dr. Holding, the Chief of Staff at the hospital, was highly sought after. Her husband would be anxious for face time, especially when she noticed the event photographer lingering nearby.

"Of course not," Jane demurred. She would never deny her husband anything.

He grinned at her and kissed her on the cheek. "Try not to get into trouble while I'm gone."

She laughed and stood watching as he disappeared across the room. They both knew trouble was the last thing she wanted.

"Jane, darling, you look simply ravishing. Is that Dior?"

Jane turned and smiled graciously as an older woman dripping in diamonds took her hand and squeezed it tightly.

"Mrs. Holding," Jane replied sincerely, taking the woman's hands in her own, "thank you. Yes, it is. Devon picked it out." Her husband would love that his choice had made an impression on the chief's wife.

"Well, it is lovely," the woman reiterated. They chatted for a moment about the gala and some events that had occurred at the hospital recently, and then Mrs. Holding sighed regretfully. "I really must go and mingle, but I would love to get together for lunch and finish catching up. Are you free next week?"

Keeping her gracious smile in place, Jane removed her hand from the woman's grip and said in her deep, modulated voice, "I'll have to check my schedule. I'll call you."

After the woman left, Jane looked around, hoping to spot her husband. Even in the crowded room, Devon was easy to spot. He stood in the middle of the room, balancing conversation between his group of peers. All attention focused on him, including the eyes of the Chief of Staff. Devon nodded and smiled at her.

Holding her gaze, Devon ever so slightly lifted his cocktail glass. His smile was bright thanks to a set of perfectly capped white teeth that radiated against his dark, tanned skin, dark hair, and dark eyes. His eyes were deep and intense and made more than one of his patients swoon when he looked at them–but Jane knew those eyes turned almost black when he was not happy.

Jane immediately noticed that the content level was too low for his liking.

With a practiced glide that belied her suddenly pounding heart, Jane moved across the room to secure her husband another drink, even though he stood not more than five feet from the bar.

It never bothered her that other wives did not accommodate their husbands as meticulously as she did. Jane was accustomed to catering to her husband, as she had for her father before that. She grew up the daughter of the CEO of the largest bank in the nation. An imposing man, he demanded nothing short of perfection from his family. Jane had learned her lessons well. Mandated ballet lessons taught her grace. Her vocal coach taught her how to control her voice to sound more quiet and well-modulated. She couldn't remember the last time she had ever raised her voice – for anything. And her manners were impeccable. She had been trained by her mother when she was very young and then by friends and companions chosen by her father to accompany her when she got older.

After her mother died, without the slightest question, she had seamlessly assumed the duties of hostess for her father's events. Most twelve-year-olds would not have known that the type of ice can make or break a premium cocktail, or that there are four different varieties of caviar. But Jane knew all of this and more.

It seemed only natural that, at eighteen, when her father introduced her to Devon Rawlings – the young cardiac specialist treating her father's heart condition – they should fall in love and get married. It had been a whirlwind romance orchestrated by her father and her fiancé. Jane had had little to do with the actual arrangements, but the wedding had made the cover of *Weddings Monthly* magazine. Shortly after they returned from a lavish honeymoon in the Bahamas, Jane's father had suffered a fatal heart attack. Devon had assumed her father's responsibilities as head of the household, managing her family's estate effortlessly. That had been ten years ago.

While her husband maintained the portfolio of assets, Jane catered to her husband in the same manner she had catered to her father. It was what her father and her husband expected; it was the only life she knew.

She strode across the room with her eyes high. The light hit her, illuminating her skin against her gown. When she reached the entourage of men surrounding her husband, Jane smiled softly in her husband's direction. She did not need to speak. Effortlessly, Jane removed the nearly empty glass from his hand and replaced it with the fresh drink she had retrieved from the bar.

"Thank you, darling," he said, leaning down to kiss her cheek. His voice was deep and masculine, just like the rest of him.

"You're welcome," she whispered in return and placed her hand on his strong jaw. Jane did not need to look back to confirm the other wives' envious stares. He was the man that every woman pictured when they thought of a successful doctor. The hours of running showcased his lean muscles. His hospital scrubs straddled every inch of his body as if he had been styled for the cover of *Men's Fashion Monthly*.

He took a sip of his drink and, pleased with the results, lifted her hand to his lips and gave her a seductive kiss on the inside of her palm, aware that his colleagues were watching with interest. "Just let me finish up here, and I'll join you in a moment."

Jane nodded with a shy half-smile and quietly slipped away from the group. She maneuvered through the crowd of her husband's colleagues and wandered toward the band, listening to the quiet instrumental music in the background, lost in her own thoughts. It didn't occur to her to approach anyone to start a conversation. There were a limited number of people her husband would be comfortable allowing her to interact with, and she was content for the moment to enjoy the surroundings on her own.

"Girl, did you see the jewels on the Chief of Staff's wife?"

Sara Brighton, the wife of Devon's colleague and good friend, Paul, grabbed Jane's arm and pulled her to the side of the room. Jane breathed a sigh of relief at the appearance of her friend.

"Where have you been?" she breathed in a whisper, careful to ensure that no one could overhear. "We've been here for over an hour."

"Paul got held up in surgery." Sara rolled her eyes. "Again. But I'm here now. What did I miss?"

Jane shrugged. "Not much, as usual. Men talking surgery; women making lunch plans; patrons writing checks." Last year, they'd raised enough money to upgrade gaming devices in every room of the children's wing and add virtual reality headsets.

Sara exhaled with an exaggerated sigh. "This is just the teaser. We both know the real money will come in during our dinner party later this month."

Jane nodded in agreement. Every year after the Grand Gala, a more intimate fundraiser occurred, usually at a private residence, where the hospital executive team wined and dined the true hospital supporters. That coveted invitation implied an unspoken competition to see who could contribute the most money, and the hospital benefited tremendously. This year, Jane and Devon were co-hosting the event with Sara and Paul at Jane and Devon's home. Jane had been working on the planning for months.

They spoke of the dinner party briefly before Sara nodded toward the bar. "Come with me. If I have to hang out in this god-awful dress all night, I can at least get a free drink out of it."

Jane smiled and followed her friend. Sara was the polar opposite of Jane, loud and flashy, with a penchant for saying exactly what was on her mind, appropriate or not. While Jane wore a conservative black dress that perfectly complimented the elegant setting, Sara had chosen a hot pink bodycon dress that hugged all of her curves, leaving little to the imagination. Devon would be appalled when he saw her, but he would be too gracious to say anything. He constantly complained to Jane about Sara's antics, but they both knew Paul liked her that way. Jane liked her, too. Living her life to the fullest without worrying about what other people thought seemed quite liberating to Jane. Not that Jane would ever let her composure slip – it was ingrained into her very soul. But it was electrifying to live vicariously through someone else occasionally.

Sara took her drink while Jane refilled on water. "I don't know how you drink just water all the time. Don't you just want a diet Coke now and then?" Sara sipped on her gin and tonic.

"I have a diet Coke," Jane protested, "now and then…" she trailed off, not even able to remember the last time she had a soda of any kind. "Besides, I need the water. You don't get skin like this without drinking eight glasses a day." She grinned and raised her chin, showcasing her perfect, clear, smooth skin.

"Oh, go on with yourself," Sara quipped. Then she snapped her fingers. "Speaking of glowing skin, are you going to go on that spa trip with me next month?"

Jane's smile faded. "I don't think I can make it."

Sara groaned and rolled her eyes. "Come on, Jane. Everything is all taken care of. Paul almost choked when I told him the cost. I made sure it has total privacy; it's very discreet. No chance of anyone seeing you in a bathing suit." She reached out and touched Jane's arm. "You know, Devon can manage a couple of days without you."

Her friend didn't even pretend there was any other reason Jane wouldn't attend. The truth was - Jane didn't really want to go to the spa and be away from her husband for that long. He depended on her for too much. There would be so much to do when she returned. And she'd be so distracted with worry, that she could never enjoy herself. It was just easier to skip. And, besides, she could have all the spa treatments she wanted right at home. Sara watched the expression on her face and said, "You didn't even ask him, did you?"

Jane hadn't, but that was none of Sara's business. "Next time," she offered simply.

"Right." Sara let out a giant, exaggerated sigh. "Next time." They both knew next time the answer would still be the same.

"Ladies." Paul and Devon joined them. They exchanged kisses all around, and Paul asked, "What are you ladies gossiping about?"

Sara opened her mouth and, afraid she would start in on the spa trip, Jane inserted smoothly, "Oh, you know, just girl talk."

Devon raised an eyebrow at her as he slipped his arm around her shoulder. His squeeze was gentle this time, but she took the hint. He wasn't a big fan of "girl talk".

"How is Dr. Holding?" she asked, laying her head against his chest, careful not to mess up her hair, and smoothly changing the topic.

"Egotistical as always," Devon replied, and Paul laughed along with him. "Talk about a God complex."

In reality, they all had God complexes. As a doctor and especially as a surgeon, their work was so tied to life and death, there was no real chance to avoid it. Jane understood it and accepted it without question. Her husband did meaningful, invaluable work and, with that, came important responsibility.

"Well, I'm glad you got to spend some time talking with him." She leaned in closer to him, enjoying the crisp, clean smell of his expensive cologne. He was solid and firm and made her feel safe, especially when he had his arms around her shoulder in such a possessive way. "I'm sure you made a terrific impression," Jane said, out of her duty to praise her husband's ego.

"He mentioned his daughter is pregnant again. I think this is her fourth," Paul added, raising an eyebrow at the group.

"That's nice, isn't it?" Jane commented while Sara made a horrified face.

"Four? That's crazy." She and Paul had a five-year-old girl and, although Paul wanted more, Sara had been putting him off.

Paul turned to Devon and Jane. "What about you guys? You two would make beautiful babies, you know."

And they would. They were each handsome individually and, physically, they complimented each other perfectly. But it was a subject never discussed in their house.

"Why would we have kids?" Devon deflected the answer without even a glance in Jane's direction. "Our life is perfect just the way it is."

Jane merely smiled, but her heart felt heavy. Devon believed children would cramp his lifestyle, but she wanted children of her own and patiently hoped one day he would change his mind.

After the party, Devon and Jane drove the short distance to their house. They lived on the top floor of a new condo development downtown. It was close to the hospital and possessed all the amenities Devon required to accommodate his lifestyle. There was a luxurious pool to swim laps in, a state-of-the-art gym for workouts any time of the day or night, and an upscale shopping center on the first floor boasting designer boutiques, a five-star restaurant, and a full-service salon and spa. It made it very easy for Jane to take care of her personal needs without having to be too far away from home.

The glass elevator made nothing more than a smooth whir as it climbed the floors to the penthouse. Jane rested her head against her husband's chest, enjoying the tranquility of the evening. At the top, the doors slid open, revealing the open modern interior of their apartment.

In whatever he did, Devon demanded the best. Their apartment was certainly that. Two stories with floor-to-ceiling glass and a million-dollar city view. The home featured two bedrooms, four bathrooms, a gourmet kitchen, a media room, and a large office for Devon. He collected art and every expensive piece was perfectly displayed to showcase its unique qualities. The floors were stained concrete. The furniture selected mid-century modern. The pièce de résistance for Devon was a floating spiral staircase connecting the upper floor to the main living area. It was fluid and practically a piece of art in its own right. Jane, personally, always felt a little cautious climbing those steps. With no railing, a misstep in her stiletto heels would be quite painful.

Devon entered the room, removed his jacket, and tossed it across the back of the sofa. Jane smiled and picked it up, carrying it to the coat closet and hanging it neatly beside the other coats lined by color. While Devon went to the bar and made himself a drink, Jane quickly made a tour of the room, straightening a pillow on the armchair, moving a vase a hair to the left, and picking up a piece of lint from the wood floor. She performed these actions as second nature. Their home had been featured in several issues of Architectural Digest and was, at any given moment, perfectly arranged should company unexpectedly drop by.

Devon took his drink into his office and shut the door. Her husband's office was the one part of the house that Jane didn't oversee. In fact, she never entered that room. Devon didn't have to keep it locked; he just clarified that it was his domain, and she was not welcome. Jane didn't question his request. Every man needed a place to escape to. Especially one that worked as hard as he did. Still, she had hoped tonight Devon would join her in the bedroom so they could talk about their evening – she had felt a certain tenderness from him this evening that was rare. She wasn't ready to let it go just yet.

Unfortunately, nothing was up to her. Devon could be in his office for fifteen minutes or two hours.

Jane sighed as she turned off the lights in the main living area and carefully ascended the floating stairs to the upper floor. The upper floor of the condo was dedicated to the master suite. The suite was enormous, with a king-sized bed that faced the twinkling city lights and stunning city views. As with the rest of the house, not an item was out of place, and Jane knew that even inside each drawer, garments were perfectly folded and aligned. She saw to that every day.

Once inside the room, Jane quickly retrieved a pair of silk pajamas for Devon and lay them across his side of the bed, then perfectly placed his slippers below them. She checked his nightstand to make sure his current reading material was available should he decide to read before bed and filled a crystal glass with fresh water to place next to it with a marble coaster. Standing at the edge of the bed, she scanned of the room. Satisfied that everything was in place, Jane made her way to the bathroom.

In keeping with the rest of the home, the master bath was spacious and elegant. Floor-to-ceiling Carrera marble adorned the main area, keeping it light and sophisticated. A huge glass shower took up a good portion of the space, but Jane's sole contribution to the bathroom had been the addition of a clawfoot tub, which sat majestically at one end of the room. It was a stunning piece and had been hell to get up the stairs, but Jane loved it.

Deciding to make the most of her time alone, Jane drew a warm bath. She added lavender salts that fizzed as they made contact with the running water and brightened the air with the soft fragrance. She unzipped her dress and hid it neatly in the dry-cleaning closet. Then she removed her jewelry one piece at a time, securing it in velvet boxes. She pinned her hair back and slid into the perfectly warm water. Relaxed by the soft scent, Jane closed her eyes and leaned back against the smooth porcelain of the tub.

While she envied the chaotic life of her friend Sara, times like this made her appreciate the luxurious life Devon provided. Of course, the money belonged to her, but Devon managed it to perfection, and they did not want for anything.

As the clock chimed, Jane drained the bathtub and wrapped herself in an oversized Turkish cotton towel. She sat at her dressing table, applying lotion to her arms and chest, when she heard Devon enter the bedroom. Her heart increased in tempo as she listened to him move about the room. In her mind's eye, she took inventory of the room. She was certain everything was in place, but sometimes Devon had other ideas.

Seconds later, apparently satisfied, Devon entered the bathroom. He moved to stand behind her and placed his hands on her shoulders. His dark eyes were dilated as he looked at her pointedly. Jane again felt her pulse quicken. She and her husband had a very active sex life. Devon was insatiable in that area, and Jane never denied him anything. She tried to gauge his mood without changing her expression. Devon's sexual appetite varied along with his mood. He could be tender and sweet or rough to the point of pain–she never knew exactly which to expect.

Jane closed her eyes as he slid the robe off her shoulders. When the movement stopped abruptly, she opened her eyes and followed his gaze down to her left forearm. There was a faint bruise visible on her pale skin, remnants of a night last week when Devon had been less than pleased with her.

Devon dropped his arms and walked back into the

bedroom, calling out over his shoulder, "I saw you talking with Glenda Holding earlier tonight."

Jane placed a hand on her burning cheeks to calm herself. Walking away from her was not a good sign. Taking a deep, shaky breath, she reached for the jar of concealer and began covering the slight blemish on her arm. Devon didn't like to be reminded of anything painful. She responded in a soothing voice, "She just stopped me for a moment."

When there was no immediate response, Jane rose quickly from the dressing table and went into her large walk-in closet. It was an oasis any woman would kill for. Easily four hundred square feet, the closet had rows of classic dresses, tailored pants, and crisp shirts hanging neatly side by side. Floor-to-ceiling dressers held her lingerie and other intimate items, and a massive shoe rack displayed rows of designer shows in every style. In the middle of the room was a freestanding armoire that held her jewelry and other accessories. Her husband was very generous with clothing and accessories. Jane rarely purchased her items, preferring instead to defer to her husband's judgment.

Opening one of the thin drawers in her dresser, Jane removed a floor-length silk gown. Devon preferred long silk gowns with spaghetti straps. She had a hundred of them in muted colors in her closet. Her husband preferred her in understated colors like lilac, mint, or blush. As a surgeon, he preferred to be the star of the show. Most of them were only worn once. She chose one in a soft lavender, one of Devon's favorite colors, in an effort to restore calm to the room. As she slid the soft silk over her head, her husband asked, "What did she want?"

His voice was muffled from the walls between them,

and she couldn't determine if he was angry or not. With her nightgown in place, she left the closet and went back to her dressing table to finish applying the Chanel No. 5 lotion he preferred. She could hear him moving about the bedroom, getting ready for bed. His movements were always precise and calculated. Although internally she made sure she was always aware of his whereabouts in case he needed something, she now sat down at her dressing table, applying lotion to her arms. "She wanted to try to have lunch next week."

There was a pause in his movements, and Jane knew he had straightened and turned in her direction. As expected, she heard his footsteps as he crossed the room and stood in the doorway to the bathroom, his gaze drilling into her. She kept her breath even and moved the lotion application to her chest.

After a moment, he asked, "What did you tell her?"

She took her time rubbing in the lotion and then turned to face her husband. He stood in the doorway, his dark gaze fixed on hers. They weren't black, but they weren't pleased, either. She smiled at him and replied, "I told her I would check my schedule and get back to her."

His jawline relaxed, and Devon smiled back. "Good - although our schedule is quite full next week. I don't think you'll be able to make it."

Of course, she wouldn't. Jane had expected nothing else. Except for Sara, Devon didn't approve of her socializing with the spouses of his colleagues. And even then, she typically only saw Sara when her husband was present. Socializing outside of the workplace was not deemed appropriate, even with the boss's wife. Jane agreed. Her life was carefully organized, and her job was taking care of her husband. It kept her very busy, and she didn't like distractions.

This time, when Devon approached her, opening his arms to her, his brown eyes sparkled, and she knew any tension had been erased.

Devon embraced her and kissed her soundly on the mouth. His lips were full and soft, and he used them with a skill that still took her breath away. He devoured her mouth with his lips and tongue and then moved his kisses from her mouth to her neck and then lower down her neckline to her chest. When a scrap of silk material impeded his progress, he simply yanked the delicate strap until it broke and the nightgown slid from her body. With a groan, he lowered his head and fastened his lips onto her exposed nipples. On some nights, he used his teeth as well, relishing the tiny bite marks remaining on her sensitive skin, but tonight his kisses were deep and succulent as he teased her nipples until they puckered, and she moaned with anticipation.

With his eyes closed and his attention focused on her body, Jane allowed herself to luxuriate in his caress. She slid her hands gently into his thick mane of hair and, when she received no complaint, closed her hands into fists, relishing the silky feeling of his hair in between her fingers. She took a deep, satisfying breath and savored the rare undivided attention of her husband. Most nights, Jane spent a considerable amount of time concentrating on his pleasure, sometimes at the expense of her own, and she was always prepared to do so. Devon's ultimate satisfaction took precedence over hers at all times, but these rare opportunities when he was the giver were a cherished occasion.

Devon was an experienced lover and knew her body so intimately. In their sexual relationship, she was always subservient to her husband's needs. It was not something that had ever been verbally discussed, it was just the way things were. Devon, without exception, dictated every aspect of their intimacy. The timing, the intensity, the methods – everything. Jane never resisted and never complained.

Tonight, he seemed to enjoy the role of giver. Jane knew better than to show an abundance of emotion. Devon preferred her to accept his gifts without show. Closing her eyes, she lay still as he moved from her breasts down her belly toward her thighs. Her insides tingled with tiny electric shocks from the featherlight kisses he planted on her sensitive skin, but she knew better than to show any reaction. He wanted to be in control, and any movement from her would distract him from his mission. She kept her fingers entwined in his hair – it was a privilege he rarely granted, and she loved the feel of his thick, soft hair around her fingers but was careful not to exert even the slightest pressure.

Nights like this, where he spent time exploring her body and caressing the most intimate parts of her in the way he knew so well, Jane felt almost grateful. His affection was like a gift to her, and she wanted to savor every second of them.

After tormenting her with kisses up and down the inside of her thighs, which were almost painful in their lightness, Devon settled down at the apex of her womanhood. He flicked his tongue down the length of her, causing a sharp intake of breath, but still, Jane remained motionless. She felt Devon smile as he continued the lazy lapping licks of her body. His tongue felt warm and soft against her, and she could feel her labia swell with anticipation. Her hips begged to rock back and forth to increase the intensity of his caress, but she forced them to remain still. Instead, the waves inside her ebbed and flowed at Devon's command. When the waves built to a crescendo inside her, Devon lifted his mouth and replaced his lips with his thumb on the center of her. He moved in a circular pattern, pushing gently to increase the pressure. Combined with the laps of his tongue, Jane's body grew frantic with need. Jane's breaths became deeper and more ragged, although she kept them quiet. She flexed her toes instead of moving her hips to create tension. She knew she was on the verge of climax and worked hard to keep it at bay.

She controlled her physical responses, concentrating instead on the intimacy of his actions knowing he liked nothing messy. She was an expert at timing her peaks to be in tune with his. Even on nights like this, she knew Devon would want things on his schedule. Jane was happy to accommodate.

Devon teased her for another agonizing minute and just when she thought she couldn't hold back any longer, he raised his head and looked at her. She opened her eyes and met his gaze, breathing slow, deep breaths. She knew her body was flushed with desire. She hoped it was the picture he expected to see.

Apparently, it was.

He moved up and kissed her on the mouth.

"What do you taste?" he asked, his voice ragged.

She took a deep breath and whispered, "Me."

He lifted his lips from hers. "Say it like you mean it." His voice had a hint of condemnation in it, indicating that her answer had not been perfect.

Not wanting to spoil the evening, she locked eyes with her husband and pulled his mouth back to hers. She kissed him soundly, and then ran her tongue over her swollen lips. She smiled and said softly but seductively, "Me. I taste me."

He smiled, parted her legs, and pushed inside her. She was already wet from his mouth and his erection slid into her like a glove. As soon as she felt the friction of him deep inside her, her insides exploded. She winced just a little as the waves of orgasm crashed through her body. Devon preferred that she orgasm with or slightly after him, but she had held back for too long already tonight. She could not hold off any longer. With a groan, Devon increased his thrusts and within a couple of minutes, exploded in a rush inside her.

Jane held tight to his back as he spent himself and then lay against her chest, panting. She feared she had rushed him into something that had not been satisfactory. She debated on whether to say something, but Devon typically preferred that she not initiate any sort of sexual conversation unless she was asked a specific question. So, instead, she waited.

A moment later, he rolled off of her but pulled her immediately to him so she could rest her head on his hard, muscular chest. He kept his arm around her shoulders and rested his chin on the top of her hair. While she couldn't see his face from her current position and didn't dare try to look up, she gathered from the relaxed, even sounds of his breath, that Devon had not been displeased at all.

The thought made Jane happy. Sex like this made her realize how lucky she was to be married to Devon. He had every quality she could want in a man and, as long as she followed the rules, life went very smoothly.

She grinned to herself, basking in the afterglow of

their lovemaking.

"What are you smiling about?" he asked.

Taking his comment as permission to move, she lifted her head and turned to face him, the smile still on her lips. "How did you know I was smiling?"

"I could feel it," he replied, a playfulness in his voice. Jane loved him like this, relaxed and happy. It allowed her to let her guard down, even for just a short time.

"What do you think I'm smiling about?" she asked.

He grinned back. "Oh, I don't know. Maybe this." He rolled her over onto her back and tweaked her distended nipple with his fingers, causing a ripple of pleasure scurrying up her spine. She gasped in surprise. "Or this." He lowered his lips onto her breast and tugged at the already sensitive area. She groaned again and laid her head back onto the pillow.

She loved the feel of his thick hair as it brushed against her chest. Her heart burst with love for her husband. His affections were hard-won, and it was brief moments like this one that renewed her faith in their relationship. Despite his rigid rules and expectations, he did have a soft side.

He looked up into her face with a smile. "What are you thinking now?"

Giving in to impulse, she bit her bottom lip and entreated softly, "Let's make a baby."

And in that instant, everything changed.

Devon's smile disappeared, and he sat up immediately and moved off of her leaving her body naked and cold in front of him. He fixed a black gaze upon her and then abruptly turned his back to her as if she sickened him.

Jane sat up and pulled the Egyptian cotton sheets over her chest. Her face, previously flushed from arousal, bore the look of embarrassment. She knew better than to bring up the taboo subject. Why had she been so careless? She had ruined everything.

"I'm sorry. I shouldn't have said that," she whispered.

Devon did not turn to look at her as he removed his robe from the leather Eames chair in the corner and swung it over his shoulders. "You're right. You shouldn't have."

His tone was curt and condescending, and Jane felt rebuked and ashamed.

"Come back to bed," she pleaded. "I didn't mean it."

Without answering, Devon went to her dressing table. He opened the top drawer where she kept her birth control pills. He grabbed the round case and stalked back to the bed. He threw the case at her, hitting her in the chest. "Take one," he demanded.

"I took it this morning," she said. "I promise." She reached for the case, holding it out to show him the empty slot.

"Take them all," he ordered, standing over her.

Jane shook her head. "I already took one. If I take any more, I'll get sick." She had a sensitive stomach and was already at the lowest dosage.

Devon reached down and grabbed her by the neck. "Take them all or so help me God I will force every one of them down your throat."

The transformation in him was complete. The tenderness of earlier had disappeared in an instant.

With tears welling up in her eyes, Jane nodded and began putting the tiny blue pills into her mouth. She would vomit all night, but that was the better alternative to Devon's wrath.

When she put the last pill into her mouth, Devon said, "Never talk to me like that again. Do you understand?"

Jane recoiled at his harsh, condescending tone. Her cheeks flamed as he regarded her with contempt. Like an errant child, she nodded in response.

"Obviously, I don't want to be around you now. Thank you for ruining my evening." With a dismissive yank on the belt of his robe, Devon departed the room.

When she heard the muffled sound of his office door shutting, Jane allowed the tears to run down her cheeks. She should be used to Devon's mood swings by now, but his patronizing, cruel behavior still stung. How could she have been so stupid? She knew how he felt about the subject. Why on earth had she brought it up?

She knew she would be sick for the rest of the evening, but she had no one to blame but herself.

It was her duty to be the perfect wife, and she had failed at her duty this evening.

She had left her husband displeased.

It was never good to leave her husband displeased.

Chapter Two

Stephanie Logan checked her watch as she turned into the back alley of her townhouse. She had completed a ten-mile run before the sun peaked through the horizon. It was nearing 7:00 a.m., one of her favorite times of the morning, just before sunrise, when the world took a moment to slow down and get ready for the day.

She had taken up running after the Leukemia Society had made a presentation to her office. Her firm sponsored a marathon training program as a fundraiser. Stephanie had lost her grandfather to leukemia when she was a child and had, in an unusual spontaneous gesture, signed up. It had been a close-knit group that had trained together, and her first marathon had been brutal, but Stephanie found running cleared her head. With her strong competitive nature, she had never been much of a team player, and she found that running allowed her to challenge herself as much, or as little, as she wanted.

Walking slowly towards her house, Stephanie rolled her neck back and forth, feeling the muscles contract and release the tension from the run. Even though the world seemed to slow down for a moment whenever she ran, her life never did. A successful real estate attorney, she lived a hectic, high-pressure life from 9 to 5. As the oldest child, she was the quintessential Type A personality, especially when it came to working. Just one of the reasons she had become a partner in her law firm at the tender age of thirty-two. Divorced and without children to distract her – she didn't even own a dog - Stephanie could focus all of her attention on her job.

And her boyfriend.

Speaking of the devil, Stephanie's heart skipped a beat when she turned into her driveway and saw a familiar Mercedes parked behind her Jeep.

Smiling, she skipped up the stairs and burst through her front door, which she always left open just for this reason.

"Devon."

He smiled at her and rose from the sofa, crossed the room, and took her into his arms. Tall and lean with powerful shoulders and long legs, the sight of him always took her breath away. She leaned in to his hug, taking a deep whiff of his crisp cologne. Like him, it smelled expensive. Everything about Devon Rawlings was expensive. The crispness of his shirt rubbed against her cheek and Stephanie sighed with pleasure. To and from work, he wore a shirt and tie, preferring to change into scrubs at the hospital. Today his tie was red, the symbol of power. Power was another word Stephanie associated with Devon. The way he carried himself, the way he spoke, the way he dressed all let people know right away he was in charge, no matter what he was doing. When he was with her, he allowed himself to relax. His life was hectic and stressful, and he always told her she provided a sanctuary in his crazy world. Now, he nuzzled the side of her neck and whispered against her ear, "Hey you."

Her smile grew softer. "Hey yourself."

It was their private greeting, and it made her heart glow every time she said it.

She stepped out of his embrace, aware she was sweaty from her run. She smiled at him, "I'm so happy to see you this morning. I wasn't expecting you." Devon normally let her know when he could stop by on his way to work in the morning. After three years of dating, she and Devon had settled into a fairly regular routine that, naturally, was subject to change due to Devon's circumstances at home. Stephanie took what she could get and made the most of the precious little time they had together. She would have preferred to be wearing something a little sexier than her running clothes, but she was happy to see him, nonetheless.

Devon reached out for her again, "I know – I should have called. I had a rough night last night and missed you."

She didn't ask what he meant by rough night. Whatever Devon was referring to was none of her business and, even if she asked, he would not share much information with her. She knew Devon was married. He had never kept that a secret. But he rarely discussed his marriage with her. In his mind, it simply had nothing to do with her.

Stephanie went to hug him but stopped mid-reach and raised a hand to her mouth, "Oh, I'm still all sweaty from my run." She knew he didn't like anything messy or dirty. "Let me go and take a quick shower."

But Devon stood, shaking his head, "I don't have much time. Don't worry - I don't mind a little sweat."

Stephanie frowned at him. Since when? He bought her expensive lotions and perfumes and encouraged her to use every ounce, and promised to buy her more if she ever ran out. He always said he loved it when she smelled soft and feminine, and he enjoyed showering her with gifts. But she suspected there was more to it than that. He simply preferred things the way he liked them.

He took her hand and tried again to pull her toward him. Stephanie hesitated, still uncomfortable with her present state. Devon stopped and stared at her. With a crooked half-smile, he said, "What? You don't believe me?"

Stephanie merely raised an eyebrow at him.

Then he smiled and raised his hands, palms forward. "You win."

Stephanie smiled and turned toward the bedroom, pulling her t-shirt over her head. "I'll only be a second."

But Devon grabbed her arm and pulled her back. "I'll do it." He lifted her shirt over her head and planted kisses down the center of her chest. "Mmmm…salty."

She pushed him away and walked into her bathroom. "That's gross."

He followed. "Nothing about you is gross."

As she adjusted the temperature of the water spray, Devon leaned against her countertop, feet crossed, smiling.

She looked at him over her shoulder as she stripped off her clothes. "Are you going to just stand there and watch?"

"As a matter of fact, I am," he said confidently.

"Wanna join me?" she asked, teasing him. He was dressed for work and would not like the idea of getting wet.

"I'm good."

Stephanie stepped into the shower. When she started to pull the shower curtain closed, he commanded, "Leave it open."

Feeling his gaze bore into her, she poured lavender-scented body wash into a large loofa. She rubbed it vigorously across her body, starting with her back.

"Slow down," he ordered, "I want you to enjoy it."

"I thought you were in a hurry," she retorted, but slowed down her movements. The feel of the luxurious lather against her wet skin did, in fact, feel good. She closed her eyes, leaned her head back, and let the warm water spray over her body. The water, just a smidge on the hot side, hit her tired muscles with a steady stream. The smell of lavender mixed with the heat of the water was a sensual, soft smell. Her muscles relaxed and her movements became languid and slow as she moved the lathered loofa over her chest and stomach in large circles.

"What does the soap feel like between your breasts?"

His voice snapped her out of her reverie. Stephanie opened her eyes and turned to him. Devon had removed his belt and stood facing her, with his pants and boxers at his ankles. His erection was thick and solid as he rubbed it with his hand. She loved the way he looked naked. She had never really thought much about the male penis, but Devon's was thick and pink covered with a soft mat of hair. She knew from experience that the thin skin around it was soft and smooth – his penis fit perfectly inside her mouth – and her vagina.

The thoughts sent a tingle across Stephanie's body. She was not shy about her sexuality. She did what she wanted, whenever she wanted, and never let anyone make her doubt her actions. It was one reason her relationship with Devon worked. Physically, they were a perfect combination.

As he continued to stroke himself in front of her, Stephanie smiled at him wickedly, ignoring his question.

She took the loofa and moved it down her chest, over her belly, and in between her legs. She moved it back and forth, feeling the friction of the mesh beneath the sweet soap working against her sensitive skin. It didn't take but a second for all the blood to rush to the area. Leaning her head against the shower wall, she found her rhythm. She dropped the loofa to the floor and used her fingers to find just the right spot, already swollen and ready. Her body immediately tightened in response. Devon might be good at a lot of things, and he was, but she knew her body better than anyone and had never been afraid to take care of her own pleasure.

"Wait…" Devon commanded from outside the shower.

His labored breathing surpassed the sound of water hitting the shower floor. He increased the rhythm of his stroking. Devon was enjoying himself as much as she was. She also knew Devon preferred to come inside her.

But it was too late. He waited too long. Her fingers moved with a will of their own. Her body had started on the path of pleasure that she could not derail.

"Damn it," Devon swore under his breath as she climaxed in the shower, but Stephanie didn't care. She loved the subtle waves caressing her insides as the water pelted her skin.

Devon panted as he continued to stroke himself. Taking pity on him, she stepped out of the shower and dropped to her knees. Replacing his swift hand motion with her soft mouth, she took him inside her and stroked firmly, keeping the same rhythm of his hand. As he filled her mouth, Devon's panting stilled, and a stroke later, he cried out and released himself to the pleasure of her mouth.

She smiled as he collapsed back onto the sink counter. "You know I would never let you down," she said.

She dried off and then tossed the towel in his direction. "I hate to end the party early, but we both can't be late for work."

She rushed past him to her room to dress, leaving the bathroom for Devon. She watched in the mirror as he tucked his crisp white shirt into his dress pants. He had a meticulous way of folding over the sides and tucking them in so that the shirt was as tight and crisp as if it were on a mannequin.

She smiled as he adjusted his tie and ran a hand through his thick, dark hair. He looked every bit the successful doctor that he was. She doubted anyone who knew him would have ever guessed he had had his pants around his ankles on her bathroom floor not ten minutes ago. She knew she would carry that memory with her for the rest of the day.

"What are you smiling at?" He grinned and gave her a kiss.

"You," she replied, but didn't elaborate. Devon's reactions were always hard to predict–she didn't know whether he would take her impression of him as a compliment or an insult. It was easier to keep it to herself.

Luckily, he was in a hurry and didn't give her response much thought. Sometimes, if he didn't like her answer, he pressed until they got into a fight over it. It was a control thing of his she didn't like. It distracted from their time together. She much preferred the simple times they shared, laughing and enjoying each other.

Giving her another kiss, he said, "Good luck with

your meeting today. I'll call you later."

She nodded and as soon as he moved through the front door, she scrambled to finish getting ready. She loved seeing Devon in the morning, but today it had put her behind, and she had an important meeting. Reluctantly, she pushed Devon from her mind and prepared for her busy day ahead.

An hour later, Stephanie sat poised and polished in the conference room of her law office on the top floor of one of the newest downtown high-rise office buildings. Across the table was a hot young attorney representing a local development company working to purchase a parcel of land in the heart of downtown. To her right, sat her client–83-year-old, David Avery, the owner of said real estate. The parcel of land being discussed had been in the Avery family for generations. It was prime real estate, and the developer was paying an exorbitant amount of money to acquire it. They were anxious to close, and Mr. Avery had been holding up the process for months. He didn't need the money and; therefore, had no sense of urgency to move the deal along. Stephanie had spent months holding his hand and explaining in great detail every nuance of the process. She knew it was his family's legacy, and she wanted him to feel comfortable throughout the negotiations.

They arrived at the final step, and Mr. Avery sat in his tweed suit and bow tie, pen in hand. His daughter and granddaughter sat on each side, watching closely. Both women had been instrumental in assisting Stephanie with the deal. In fact, they had personally sent a driver and car to pick up Mr. Avery and bring him to the building. With a shaking hand, Mr. Avery positioned the pen over the bound contract. It hovered for a moment.

The entire room, except for Stephanie, leaned forward in anticipation. Mr. Avery turned his head to look at Stephanie, his bushy grey eyebrows raised in question. Stephanie smiled at him.

"I just want to look at one thing," he started, his voice creaking with age, but still sounding strong and in control.

"Oh, for Christ's sake," the young attorney slammed his pen on the table. "What now?"

Stephanie shot the broker a look and said in a deliberately low voice that meant no nonsense. "Would you excuse us for a moment?"

The broker clenched his jaw, and she saw a tiny vein pop out on his forehead. Stephanie sat back in her chair, crossed her legs beneath her slim pinstriped pencil skirt, and placed her manicured hands primly on the table, waiting.

"Can't we just talk about whatever the problem is now?" the attorney asked aggressively, his tone revealing his irritation at the additional delays.

Mr. Avery cleared his throat as if to speak, but Stephanie placed her hand on top of his, keeping her gaze focused on the gentlemen sitting across the table. She wasn't about to let her client be intimidated by anyone.

Lowering her voice to an almost whisper, she directed, "My client and I would like a moment alone, please."

After a lengthy staring contest, the attorney sighed loudly. "Fine. We'll be right outside."

The gentlemen practically stomped out of the room like toddlers, while Mr. Avery's granddaughters gave him a kiss on the cheek and followed quietly.

Once the door shut firmly in place, Mr. Avery

chuckled. "I do like to watch you work. Reminds me of myself at that age."

Stephanie took that as the most sincere of compliments. He had had some doubts initially about working with a female attorney, but Stephanie was anything but typical. Even though women had made all kinds of progress in the industry over the years, it was still, at its core, a "good old boy" operation. Stephanie didn't let people's attitudes stop her from establishing a stellar reputation with one of the most successful real estate law firms in the city. No one could negotiate better than Stephanie. She never ever lost her temper professionally. She had learned that lesson early from her boss who had taken a risk on her early in her career. He had taught her that the higher the pressure cooker, the less reaction she should show. React in the opposite manner, no matter what the situation. It threw off the opponent every time. After watching her mentor complete high-profile deal after deal using that exact technique, it had become almost an obsession with her. Now, years later, she was an expert and on the brink of closing the largest deal of her career. Although the commission to the firm, and ultimately to her as well, would be significant, for Stephanie, the thrill was in completing a deal in the best interest of her client. She knew money meant little to the developer in the other room, but taking care of his family meant everything to Mr. Avery.

She turned to her client with a smile. "That means a lot to me. Now, what did you want to go over?"

Mr. Avery's smile turned mischievous. "Nothing. I just wanted to see that little guy squirm one last time."

It was not nice, and Stephanie shouldn't laugh,

though she wanted to. "Mr. Avery..." she started.

"Okay, okay," he held up a hand. "I'll make it legitimate. Bring those whippersnappers back in here and let's get this thing done."

Stephanie grinned. She was going to miss working with Mr. Avery. For a while anyway. The family still owned one of the largest real estate portfolios in downtown Miami. She had a feeling they would work together again.

As the opposing attorney and his clients reentered the room, the young man looked ready for a fight, but Mr. Avery played his last card and signed the documents without further delay. Stephanie leaned over and gave him a warm hug and, a moment later, his daughter and granddaughter escorted him from the room.

The developers signed the rest of the documents, and Stephanie handed them over to her paralegal for final processing.

"It's about time," the attorney groused as he replaced his documents into his briefcase.

"It's a good deal for everyone," Stephanie replied diplomatically.

Sensing it was best to stay in her good graces, the man rose and offered his hand. "Thank you for your help."

"You're welcome." Stephanie stood and shook his hand. Her grip was as firm as any man's. Another tip from her mentor. If you're playing in a man's world, have a firm handshake.

She walked the men through the large conference room, into the reception area, and out to the elevator lobby. The men were all dressed alike in conservative suits and power ties. While she might negotiate like a man, Stephanie drew the line at dressing like one. Today she wore a black pinstriped skirt with a tailored white ruffled blouse that showed just a touch of cleavage. It was completely professional, yet feminine. Like Stephanie.

When the elevator began its smooth descent from the 21st floor to the lobby, Stephanie let out an audible sigh and turned to her paralegal, Kate. "We did it."

Kate gave her a hug and a big grin. "Yeah, we did." Kate had played an important role in getting the information to and from Mr. Avery since he didn't drive. Stephanie glanced down at her watch. It was after 2:00 PM. They had been working on the deal since 10:00 AM. She grinned at Kate. "I have an idea. Why don't we gather up the team, and anyone else who wants to go, and meet down at Joe's for a beer in about an hour?"

It had been a great day for her, starting with the surprise visit from Devon and ending with a successful business transaction. It would have been nice to celebrate with Devon, but that was not an option while he was married. But her team deserved to celebrate the victory today.

Joe's, a small bar located a block away from her office building, catered mostly to a local crowd. It had a wonderful selection of beer, and the bartender never missed a beat.

Stephanie sipped on a lite beer and grinned as her counterparts told stories of real estate transactions gone bad. She had her share of stories as well, but for the moment, was content to just sit and listen.

"Looks like your beer is running low."

A young man in a suit pointed at her glass as she looked up from the table. "Can I get you another one?"

The well-dressed man was fairly attractive in that clean-cut way she preferred. The thought fled her mind. She shook her head and said, "I'm good, thanks."

"You sure?" the guy asked, giving her a curious grin. Stephanie wasn't surprised. With his looks, he probably wasn't turned down often.

She gave him a regretful smile that did not reach her eyes. "I'm sure."

He didn't put up any further argument. Instead, he offered a smile and said, "Let me know if you change your mind."

As he turned his back and walked away, she forgot the last time she let someone buy her a drink. It had been over five years since her divorce, but she didn't feel any closer to being ready to date than the day her husband left her. She had married her high school sweetheart just after college. It had not entered her mind that her husband, the only man she had ever been with, would leave her for another woman on their fifth wedding anniversary. Not only had she been crushed and humiliated, but did not know what to do with herself. Her entire identity from the time she was sixteen had been as one-half of a couple. She immersed herself into work– learning the ropes and ascending the ladder at her firm.

Devon had entered her life at the perfect time. Still wounded from the betrayal of her husband, Stephanie had been emotionally depleted. Devon had offered affection and companionship, with no emotional commitment. Back then, it had felt like the perfect solution. He came and went, leaving her alone most of the time. The sex was great and their encounters, brief as they were, were full of passion and excitement. She was at the top of her game at work. For now, that was enough.

With a traditional relationship, her career might suffer.

Deep down, in her heart, she knew being with Devon was not a long-term solution for her. But he loved her, and she was comfortable with their routine.

"Looks like you could use this." One of her colleagues, Brad Jenson, slid a beer in front of her and took the seat next to her. "What are you doing sitting here all by yourself?"

For the first time, Stephanie looked around to realize the rest of her group had moved over to the pool tables while she had been reflecting on her loneliness. She hadn't even noticed them leave.

"Just a lot on my mind."

Brad smiled. "Everything okay?"

Stephanie contemplated the full beer sitting in front of her. Part of her wanted to refuse the drink, pay her tab, and go home. She looked down at her watch. It was past 4:00. She could get home in plenty of time to watch the evening news. No one, except for Brad, would even notice.

"Hey," he touched her shoulder. "We're celebrating your win, remember? You should be having fun not sitting here by yourself moping."

She looked up at Brad. He watched her with an earnest expression as if he were truly concerned about her wellbeing. And in fact, that might be true. They had been colleagues for several years and he was always asking how she was doing or offering to help her in some way. She had never given it much thought, but he was probably one of those people who you could trust and rely on. She had been too preoccupied to notice.

She shrugged. "I'm not moping."

Brad raised an eyebrow in clear disbelief.

A quiet burst of laughter escaped her lips. "Well, I mean, I wasn't moping earlier."

"What happened then?" Brad sat back in his seat but kept his attention on her.

"This guy wanted to buy me a drink," she started to say and then realized how ridiculous that sounded and wished immediately she could take it back.

Too late. Brad burst into laughter. "I can see how that would be upsetting." He shook his head in mock disgust. "Some people just don't know when they are crossing the line." He reached over and slid the beer out from in front of her. "I'll just take this back. I wouldn't want to send you into a full-fledged state of depression."

Stephanie grabbed the beer and took a large swig. "It's okay. I'm over it now."

"Oh, I see," Brad said, pretending to sound hurt. "I'm not good enough to cause panic and depression."

Stephanie laughed and tilted her head to look at him. For the first time, she noticed the kindness in his eyes. She rarely took the time to sit back and observe her surroundings. It was one of her weaknesses .She was always on full alert and focused on the next project. Brad had just as full of a caseload as she did, yet he always had the scoop on who had been out sick or who had a new boyfriend. The girls in the office were always commenting that he brought in cookies, sometimes homemade, or breakfast tacos and shared funny stories about his dog, a pug named Emmitt, whom he adored whenever the subject of kids came up. He was a genuinely nice guy, and suddenly Stephanie was grateful he had joined her.

Now, she raised her glass and said sincerely, "Thanks for the beer."

He smiled at her, revealing a set of even white teeth. "Thanks for not telling me to get lost. I didn't want to tell you this before, but I saw that guy you rejected crying in the bathroom."

Stephanie felt her eyes widen for a split second before she recognized the gleam in his eye. He was pulling her leg.

"Ha Ha," she quipped. She took another sip. "So," she ventured, grasping for a suitable topic of conversation. Suddenly, another weakness reared its ugly head. She was terrible at small talk. "Uh…" Suddenly, dumbstruck, she forgot what she planned to say next. She could go toe to toe with her male peers all day and night, but when a genuinely nice guy sat next to her, she had nothing to say. No wonder she didn't date.

Brad let her off the hook. "Go ahead, ask me anything. I have nothing to hide. Hook me up to a lie detector if you have to."

She froze. Brad might have nothing to hide, but Stephanie had plenty of skeletons in her closet.

As if on cue, her cell phone vibrated, rescuing her from herself. She glanced down at the number and felt her heart skip a beat.

It was him.

Standing so abruptly, her beer sloshed over the side of her glass, she said flustered, "I need to take this…"

Brad nodded. "I'll wait…."

But Stephanie shook her head, already making her way towards the front door. "I probably won't be back. I'll talk to you tomorrow."

"Is everything okay?" he asked as she moved away from the table. Without turning back, she nodded and held up her hand to indicate that it was. She would apologize tomorrow for her abrupt behavior. Pushing through the heavy front door of the bar, Stephanie jogged out onto the sidewalk where the music from inside the bar couldn't be heard. She pushed the talk button on her phone just as the fourth ring was underway. She didn't want the call to go to voicemail.

"Hello?" She struggled to keep the breathlessness from her voice.

"I'm at your condo."

Her world sped up to hyper mode. She mentally calculated the time it would take to get back to her car and then make it home and subtracted ten minutes. "I'll be there in ten minutes."

Nine minutes later, she pulled into her driveway next to the black Mercedes parked in her spot. She gave herself thirty seconds to take a couple of deep breaths and apply powder to her cheeks. She was exhausted from her whirlwind day but didn't want it to show. Exactly ten minutes after she ended her call, she opened the front door to her condo and walked in.

Devon stood up and greeted her in the foyer.

"Twice in one day," she said with a smile. "To what do I owe this pleasure?"

"I missed you," he growled, tearing at the buttons on her silk shirt before she even had a chance to set down her briefcase. "And we didn't get to have proper sex this morning."

It didn't take much for Stephanie to respond. Devon was such a passionate kisser that, even in her state of exhaustion, she felt her body react to his touch with an urgency that never diminished.

She groaned against his chest. "Watching me come doesn't count as proper sex?"

"Not unless I'm inside you," he responded without missing a beat.

Devon guided her into the bedroom and lay her down on the bed. He pushed the pencil skirt up to her waist and removed her lace panties. He held them up and let them dangle from his index finger. "This is what you wear to work beneath that grown-up business suit?"

She laughed. "Ironic, huh?"

He raised an eyebrow. "I thought you only wore nice things for me. Should I be jealous?"

She snatched the garment from his hand and threw it across the room. "I wear nice things for myself. Now put your dick inside me before I come without you– again."

He stepped away from her, his eyes darkening as he stared at her. "One day, my love, you will learn not to test my patience."

There was the hint of a threat in his tone, but, as he removed his boxer briefs, she could see his full erection, so she knew that her words had aroused him. She pushed the implied threat to the back of her mind.

He knelt between her legs and slid his fingers inside her. She was wet and slippery and completely ready for him. She heard his sharp intake of breath as he moved his fingers inside her sleek womanhood. "I love when you are so ready for me," he growled.

"Don't talk - just fuck."

With another sharp intake of breath, he removed his fingers and jammed his cock inside her, filling her with its thickness. She exploded instantly.

He continued his rhythmic thrusts. She knew he loved making her come. She was never shy about expressing her pleasure–luckily, for him, she was easy to please. She allowed her waves of pleasure to build and flow with his motion, basking in the aftershocks of her orgasm. Within minutes, he shouted, and with one last thrust, emptied himself inside her.

Spent, Devon rolled over and lay next to her. He rested his head on one hand and smiled at her. "Hey you," he said in his deep, sexy voice.

She smiled back. "Hey, yourself."

She gave him a quick kiss and then slid out of the bed and reached for a pair of shorts and a t-shirt before asking casually, "Can you stay?" She never pushed.

He got out of bed and put his arms around her waist, kissing the back of her neck. "For a little while."

"Are you hungry?"

He nodded and followed her into the kitchen. She reached into the pantry and pulled out a box of pasta. Her idea of a gourmet meal consisted of take-out delivered from a restaurant down the street. Most nights, she feasted on a salad or leftovers from lunch. Luckily for her, Devon was not picky. He moved to the fridge and grabbed the lettuce and tomatoes, and started chopping vegetables for a salad. He was an excellent cook, and it made her happy to stand side by side with him in her small kitchen preparing dinner. Like any couple in love.

Only they weren't any couple.

Devon put the salad on the counter and took an open wine bottle from the fridge. Stephanie kept his favorites on hand for evenings just like this. She wanted him to feel at ease in her home, even though it was barely a quarter of the size of his penthouse. She had never been to his place, of course, but it had been featured in Architectural Digest, and she kept a copy in her nightstand. It impressed her that despite the level of luxury he was accustomed to, he always acted perfectly at home in her apartment.

He poured her a glass of wine and handed it over her shoulder as he pressed against her back. "Mmmm... Smells delicious."

She took the glass and sipped the rich, red wine. "It's pasta. With store-bought pesto sauce. You know my culinary skills are a little lacking."

"Your skills are perfect," he responded immediately, trailing butterfly kisses down her arm. "You proved that just a few minutes ago."

"Stop." She giggled, stirring the pasta. "How was your day?"

Devon sighed dramatically and leaned against the island in her kitchen. "Same as always. Heart transplant here. Pulmonary disorder there."

"Sounds terribly monotonous," she quipped. "How do you manage?"

He shrugged, his eyes twinkling. "Ah, you know, someone's gotta do it." Then he drained the last of his wine. "Want more?" he asked as he reached for the bottle and filled both of their glasses. "Seriously, though, I wish the Chief of Staff would recognize the progress I've made with developing that new pulmonary stint. It could revolutionize the way we perform that surgery."

"Have you shown it to him?"

Devon nodded. "He wants me to write up a paper and submit it to the medical journal. Get some backing before we go to prototype."

"Sounds reasonable. A positive write-up in the medical journal would be a good thing to have on your resume."

"You're right," Devon agreed. "It just takes so long

to complete the progress."

"And patience is not one of your strong suits," Stephanie countered, "but this time, I think it would be worth it." She leaned back and kissed him. "I think you're marvelous, you know."

She loved it when he shared stories from his day with her. It made her feel important in his life. He always told her he didn't have anyone else to talk to.

"How about you?" Devon asked. "Anything exciting happen today?"

"We sold that building," she offered, unable to hide the pride in her voice.

"You did? That's great." He seemed genuinely happy for her. "How was Mr. Avery?"

Stephanie shrugged. "I think he felt a little sad. But he knew it was the right thing for him and his family. It was important to me, as well, to make sure he and his family were taken care of."

Devon was a skilled listener and seemed impressed with the complexities of her job. The more he asked, the more she wanted to share.

"And I know you did the absolute best job possible," he complimented. "You're an amazing attorney." He gave her a kiss and said softly, "I'm proud of you."

"Thanks," she said, serving up the simple plates of pasta and salad.

"You know," he commented as they headed toward her small dining table, "I was worried when you weren't here when I arrived."

Stephanie frowned, stopping her tracks, and turned in his direction. "Why would you be worried? I'm never here this early."

"I know, but when I called your office, you didn't

answer, so I assumed you were on your way home." Devon's tone had turned just a shade petulant, and Stephanie felt a tinge of irritation. She didn't like the fact that he checked up on her so often, and even though he had before in the past, every once in a while, it bothered her.

Now, she shrugged and set her plate on the table, heading back to the kitchen for the bottle of wine. "I was out with the group at Joe's, celebrating the sale."

"Oh." His eyes grew a shade darker as he followed her progress. "I hope no one got too friendly with you."

"Don't be ridiculous," she protested, returning and leaning around him to place the bottle on the table. "Those are my colleagues."

"Well, I don't like the idea of all those men being so close to you." He reached around her waist and pulled her to him. "I might get jealous."

Which was interesting since he had a wife.

Stephanie accepted the hug but didn't respond. After a long moment, he released her and together they sat down to eat. Dinner passed without further comment, but Stephanie noticed Devon glancing at his watch. She had expected him to eat quickly and be on his way, but by the time the last of the wine had been finished, it was close to 8:00.

"I need to get going," Devon finally said, already pushing back from the table.

Stephanie nodded. 8:00 was late for him. He must have been exceptionally concerned about other men hitting on her. He always gave her extra attention when he felt insecure. She smiled at him and murmured, "I'll miss you tonight."

"Me, too. Thanks for dinner." He gave her a

lingering kiss. As always, a tinge of sadness hit her when he reached for his suit jacket. Three hours with him was much longer than usual, but she felt lonely when he left.

As he kissed her one last time in the doorway, he called out, "I'll call you later."

Stephanie shut the door and leaned against it. Her small apartment felt empty. Maybe she should get a dog for companionship.

Stephanie shook off the melancholy. She was lonely because Devon was gone. She reminded herself that her life was rewarding and full.

Feeling restless, Stephanie changed into running clothes. A short run to burn off her excess energy from being with Devon would be just the thing to get her mind straight. She was happy with her life and didn't need nagging thoughts of him bringing her down.

After her run, Stephanie took a relaxing shower and changed into a hot pink silk cami set. She wasn't above lounging around the house in her most comfy PJs, but Devon loved sexy, silky lingerie, especially in bright vibrant colors, and she had gotten into the habit of wearing something silky every evening. Sometimes on the phone he asked what she was wearing and it turned both of them on to hear her describe in detail the tiny scraps of silk that adorned her body. The only thing Devon didn't allow was long silk nightgowns–he said they reminded him of an old lady.

She had just settled down to watch some reality TV when her phone rang. She glanced at her watch.

9:55. Devon normally called right around 10:00.

She picked up the phone with a smile. "Hello?"

"Come back to Joe's," the voice on the other line prodded in a rush.

Expecting to hear Devon's quiet, sexy voice, the exuberant voice on the other end threw her for a loop initially. And then she realized who it was. "Brad?"

"Yeah," he said.

"You're still there?" He'd have one hell of a hangover tomorrow.

"You ran out in such a hurry. Come back for a little while."

Stephanie couldn't help but smile. He sounded like a little boy pleading for his friend to come out and play. He had a great phone voice. Smooth and deep and very appealing.

"I can't," she said, looking at her watch again. It was getting close to 10:00. She did not want to explain why she was on the other line when Devon called. "I have to go."

"No, wait…," Brad began, but she cut him off. "I'll talk to you tomorrow."

She hung up the phone precisely at 10:00.

The quiet in her house was suddenly overwhelming. Here she was, a grown, independent woman, sitting alone in her house waiting for the phone to ring.

Stephanie stood up and paced the room. At 10:05, she felt her irritation escalate. There was a part of her that wanted to go back and join her friends. She missed the interaction with people her age. Single people her age. She spent most her evenings at home–waiting for the phone to ring.

She glanced down at the apparatus in her hand. It was a blessing and a curse to her. She supposed she could keep her cell phone with her and go out anyway, but she knew Devon would know instantly that she was not at home and question what she was doing. And then she would feel bad. Devon was good at making her feel bad about things like that. Even if he had no right to. She knew she had no reason to feel guilty for going out and certainly shouldn't allow him to make her feel that way.

Still, it was easier to just sit and wait. She could always go out another time.

At 10:15, the phone rang.

She picked it up on the first ring. "Hello?"

"Hey you." His deep, sexy voice, always almost a whisper at this hour made her heart race.

She sank down onto the sofa. "Hey yourself."

"How was the rest of your evening?"

She pushed aside the nagging irritation and said simply, "My evening was fine. I went for a run and then watched some TV and got caught up on some emails. How about yourself?"

There was the slightest hesitation, and then he replied, "Nothing special."

She always wondered what that meant. Did he and his wife just sit around and say nothing all night and go to bed in silence? But she knew better than to press. It was none of her business, anyway.

Devon cleared his throat and said curtly, "I need to get going." Whatever "nothing special" clearly occupied the forefront of his mind.

Stephanie looked down at her watch. Three minutes. She had wasted an entire evening sitting around for a three-minute conversation. It was almost as if all Devon wanted was to make sure she was home–alone.

As she formulated a response, she heard him admit, "You know, these conversations make my evenings bearable. I don't know what I would do without them."

Right. He said that all the time as well. As if his very

happiness was dependent on her availability. The tremendous responsibility was unfair to put on her.

She said goodbye and pressed END on her phone. Her heart felt heavy as she climbed into bed, but she fell asleep almost immediately. It had been a long day, and her body was exhausted. Her mind; however, continued to play tricks on her even as she slept. In her dreams, she was out of the house at a store shopping when she realized she didn't have her phone with her. Her heart started to pound with irrational fear. She looked at her watch. It read 10:00.

Oh, no, I'm going to miss the call...

I'm going to miss the call...

Stephanie searched frantically through her purse, but the phone was nowhere. She was sweating, and her knees felt as if they would buckle beneath her. Her breaths were coming in short, ragged gasps.

He's going to be angry...

He's going to be angry...

Stephanie sat bolt upright in bed. Her body was covered in perspiration, and her chest literally felt sore from gasping. She glanced over at the clock on her nightstand. Midnight. Closing her eyes, she attempted to calm her breathing, thinking back. Yes, she had talked to Devon this evening. Everything was fine.

It was not the first time Stephanie had had what she referred to as "the dream." She often had variations of it– always resulting in the loss of her cell phone when Devon's call was due. It was ridiculous, she knew. The power Devon held over her was dangerous.

Stephanie lay back in bed, pulling the covers to her chin, but sleep wouldn't come easily this time around. Thoughts of Devon tormented her mind.

They weren't even involved in a real relationship. She couldn't talk about him to any of her friends. She didn't dare talk about him at all. If even a hint got out, it would be devastating to him. She was surprised there weren't rumors in the office about her sexuality. She never talked about her personal life, but surely, someone in her position should be dating, at least. How long would she be able to milk the "I'm not over my divorce" excuse?

Still, it was hard to imagine life without Devon. The little time they spent together was magical, even now. Devon occasionally had whisked her away to New York or even Los Angeles for dinner. Granted, they never flew together, and she had paid for her own airfare. But the dates were exciting and romantic. Devon was charming and attentive. Not to mention the fact the sex was always spectacular. When she was with Devon, she felt special. Most of the time that feeling made up for his possessiveness; but, deep down, she recognized that while, technically, Stephanie had no commitment to Devon, she felt as bound to him as she had ever felt when she was married.

Without any of the benefits of being married.

She should get out of the relationship. It had run its course, and it wasn't healthy. Devon would never leave his wife–he had said many, many times that she was dependent on him financially and emotionally. He described her as quite a fragile woman, and he felt responsible for her. And, honestly, Stephanie wasn't even certain she liked him for who he was or just because he was predictable. She knew what she was getting and when she was getting it. No more; no less.

She had taken risks before that did not work out as

she had envisioned. Devon was safe. Maybe that was all she needed in a partner.

Chapter Three

When Jane awoke the next morning, her head felt heavy from tossing and turning. Her stomach rolled from the nausea that had set in once the pills started to dissolve.

She had heaved until she had nothing left in her stomach and then dry heaved some more. She had suffered in silence because to rouse Devon back upstairs would have been much worse. She didn't know where he went, but he had not been back upstairs all evening.

As she slid out of the warm bed, Jane glimpsed at her discarded silk nightgown on the floor. She picked it up on the way to the bathroom, fingering the delicate material. A broken strap was an easy enough fix for the tailor, but Jane knew Devon would not want to see the garment again. She tossed it into a wicker basket inside of her closet to be donated to charity.

Quickly, she wrapped a thick silk robe over her naked body, brushed her teeth and hair, and made her way downstairs into the kitchen. If Devon was up, he would want breakfast before he left for work. He would not want to see any sign of her restless night. She had to always look perfectly put together, no matter how she felt on the inside.

She padded across the spacious living room into the large modern kitchen, separated from the living area by a ten-foot long island. As she turned on the lights, she noticed the piece of paper sitting on top of the island.

Too late.

Devon had already been here.

With a sigh, Jane picked up the meticulously written note. Devon had left a list of instructions for her day.

Pick up dry cleaning–make sure to inspect the shirts. Last time there was a wrinkle on the blue-striped shirt

Pick up a bottle of wine at the store–a good bottle this time

Prepare a menu for next Saturday's dinner party–I will review when I get home

Don't forget–it's trash day

Hair appt - 10:00 AM

There were several other items on the list, and Jane read over the items and then placed the note in the pocket of her robe. It didn't occur to her to be offended in any way. Devon had learned the list technique from her father, who had left her similar lists since she was fifteen.

She spotted a damp towel draped over the suede chair.

She reached for it and sighed at the dark spot left on the back of the chair. She moved into the laundry room and placed the towel on top of the washing machine. Reaching into the cabinet, she removed a can of upholstery spray and a clean cloth. She quickly sprayed the fine foam spray and then dabbed at it with the clean cloth until she felt confident any spot or stain that could have been left had been properly removed.

The house phone rang just as Jane finished putting away the cleaning supplies.

"Hello?"

"Yes, Ms. Rawlings, your driver is here." The voice on the other end was that of the building concierge, sounding respectful, if not at all interested in her comings and goings.

"My driver?" Jane looked down at her silk robe. "I didn't ask for a driver this morning."

"Yes, ma'am, your husband called for one. He said you had a busy day."

"Right." Jane closed her eyes. How many times had she hinted to Devon that she preferred to plan her own day? But he was always concerned she wouldn't be able to get everything done and insisted she take a driver. That was another source of contention between them. Jane had her very own Mercedes sedan parked in one of the two very expensive spaces of the building garage, but Devon never let her drive it. He said it was much too dangerous for a woman to be driving around town alone. He preferred knowing she was safe with his driver, George, who, although he was perfectly nice and completely professional, made it very clear to Jane that he worked for Devon.

There was no sense in arguing with him.

"I'll be down in ten minutes," she said with a sigh and replaced the receiver.

Instead of the leisurely morning she had anticipated, Jane was forced to quickly apply her makeup at the dressing table. Luckily, she rarely wore a great deal of it, so the process was not time-consuming. She hurried into her closet and grabbed a pair of navy slacks with a crisp white shirt. It was her go-to uniform for times like this. No matter what kind of hurry she was in–it would be unacceptable to be seen in public looking anything less than perfectly put together. She accessorized the outfit with a gold Cartier bangle bracelet and her favorite pair of diamond stud earrings.

On the way out, she grabbed her yoga bag, which thankfully she kept packed. With any luck, she'd be able to squeeze in a class while she was out.

Nine minutes after the phone rang, Jane strolled through the lobby of the building and out the glass doors, where she was promptly helped into a Black Lincoln Town Car parked at the entrance. She felt peoples' gaze on her as the driver made a fuss over whether she was comfortable. Once people realized she wasn't a celebrity, they rolled their eyes at her extravagance. It made Jane uncomfortable, but she knew there was no use in arguing the matter. Devon was set on it and nothing she could say would change his mind.

George consulted his notes and announced, "We'll stop by the dry cleaners first and then head over to the grocery store."

"Actually," Jane began, and George looked at her sharply. She almost buckled under his stare, but managed to stand her ground, stating firmly, "I have a hair appointment at 10:00." When George opened his mouth to argue, she said first, "Devon made the appointment–it should be on the schedule." She felt like a child having to explain herself like that, but it was better than arguing.

"With Reba?" George asked. Jane perceived as a touch of suspicion in his voice. As if she would dare to make an appointment with anyone else. Reba had been doing her hair since she was a young girl. Reba had done her mother's hair before her. However, Reba's loyalty, much like Georges, rested solely with Devon. It was Devon who scheduled her appointments when he thought Jane's hair needed a trim. The one time Jane had suggested to Devon that she try the salon in their building for the sake of convenience, he had become so insulted she thought he might burst a blood vessel. "I will not allow some young tramp wearing black leather and a nose ring to put their hands on you," he had screamed, turning red in the face. Jane hadn't bothered to inform him that the salon was so upscale, the stylists wore white lab coats and were completely professional.

Now Jane merely sighed. "Of course with Reba."

George consulted his notes again and then acquiesced, "Very well."

Garbo was an upscale salon inside a high-end retail center near the condo. It was decorated with floral prints and high-backed chairs. The walls were dark paneled wood and the workstations heavy and massive. If it felt like it had been transported from the 1940s, that was because it was tailored to suit its clientele. Garbo catered to the more mature women living in the nearby neighborhood. Jane immediately felt thirty years older as soon as she entered the salon. It even held the faint musty smell of mothballs that she associated with the palatial homes lining the streets.

As they pulled up to the curb, George jumped from the driver's seat and came around to open the door and escort her from the car. Instead of making her feel special, it only served to make her feel feeble and unable to get herself out of an automobile. It was just one more thing she disliked about these trips.

As soon as she entered the building, Reba came out and embraced her warmly. The woman was easily 60 years old and had bright orange hair and wore too much makeup, but she was nice enough and always gave Jane a style Devon approved of.

The two women air-kissed, and Jane followed Reba back to her station. As Reba began laying out her styling tools, Jane debated on whether to mention the ad she had in her purse. She had worn her hair in the same slick shoulder-length bob since she had known Devon. He liked it because it was sleek and sophisticated. But just the other day, she had seen a magazine ad showing a woman with similar features to hers wearing a slightly tousled bob of a similar length and general style, only with more youth and fun. Jane thought it might look good on her. After all, she was twenty-nine, not eighty. She hadn't had a chance to mention it to Devon but had stuffed the picture in her purse as a reminder.

Reaching for her bag to show the picture to Reba, she said quietly, "You know, I was thinking I might like to add a few layers this time."

Reba paused, holding a pair of styling sheers mid-air. "What did you say?"

A pin drop could be heard in the salon at that instant.

Jane was certain she could hear the pounding of her heart. But she had started the conversation, and she wanted to finish it. It wasn't like she asked the woman to dye her hair purple, for goodness' sake. Sliding out the magazine page, she showed it to Reba. "See? It's basically the same cut, with just some layers at the bottom for volume."

Reba studied the picture. "What does Devon think?"

Jane bristled at the assumption. She was a grown woman, after all. She could certainly make decisions regarding her own hair. "I think Devon would like this look on me."

"So, you haven't told him?"

Jane stubbornly refused to answer.

Reba nodded and then asked, "Will you excuse me for just a moment?"

Jane sighed as the woman dropped her sheers on the tray and scurried away. Jane pinched her lips together and watched in the reflection of the mirror as Reba practically ran to the reception desk and reached for the phone.

She's calling Devon. Jane's face flushed with humiliation at the thought that Reba felt it necessary to call her husband as if she were an errant child.

She was even more humiliated when Reba returned with a smile and said smugly, "I think we'll just stick with the usual bob today."

Of course, Devon had nixed her request.

Jane folded the picture up and placed it back in her bag.

Thirty minutes later, looking exactly the same as when she entered the salon, Jane slid back into the Lincoln.

"Your hair looks very nice," George commented as he pulled away from the curb.

Still bristling over the whole incident, Jane refrained from replying. While she accepted the fact that Devon liked to be in control of every aspect of his life, including his wife, sometimes it stung more than others. After all, Jane was an intelligent woman. She had been accepted to an Ivy League college and had planned to study education – the only subject her father would allow her to study. She had accepted the decision and had excelled in her studies. Jane once believed she would have been a wonderful teacher. Until Devon came along. It had been clear that Devon, like her father, expected his wife to stay home and run the household. Having a job outside the home had never been an option for her. Still, she was perfectly capable of making an intelligent decision about a haircut.

Jane felt stifled driving away from the salon. She didn't care about Devon's stupid schedule. She needed a release.

"I would like to attend the 11:30 Yoga class at the club," she announced firmly. Yoga at the private gym she and Devon belonged to was on the "approved" list, and she didn't have to get permission to go. It was one of the few luxuries she was allowed.

"But, ma'am," George objected immediately, "we have a very busy day today."

"I have a busy day," she corrected, more stringently than she intended. "And I want to go to yoga first. Now, please take me to the club." She knew she sounded like a spoiled, rich wife, but she wanted to do something without having to beg for once.

George pinched his mouth shut and flipped on the turn signal.

Jane smiled from her place in the back seat.

Oh, sure. She'd hear about it later on. As soon as she stepped foot out of the car, George would call her husband and report how insubordinate she had been. Coupled with the call he had already received from Reba this morning, Devon was certain to be unhappy with her for disrupting that much of his day. It would not be a pretty conversation. And she would more than likely pay for it in the bedroom that evening.

But right now, she just didn't care. She wanted to do something on her own and by god, this was it.

This time, George did not escort her from the car. Unlike her, there would be no repercussions for his behavior.

Jane took her bag and entered the club with a smile.

What she wanted to do was walk straight through to the back entrance and hail a taxicab. For a brief second, she allowed herself to imagine the glorious freedom of being able to go anywhere she wanted–by herself. Just throw out an address and be taken there–without question. She sighed out loud. As amazing as that sounded, she knew it certainly wasn't worth the price that would have to be paid.

"Are you headed over to the modern hip-hop class?"

A tall young man in spandex workout clothes eyed her with a friendly smile. Jane followed his gaze through an open door into a room full of young people stretching and murmuring. There was an energy radiating from the room that Jane could feel run through her. How fun would it be to join that group and let herself go to the upbeat rhythm?

Jane slid her gaze towards the front door of the gym. George was most likely in the car, reading the Wall Street Journal. He would never know which class she attended.

She turned her attention back to the man beside her. He smiled his encouragement. "Tyra is teaching today. She's the best."

His enthusiasm was contagious, and Jane found herself smiling back at him. "It sounds like a great class."

"It is." He nodded his head. "Come on–join us." Then he shrugged in a carefree manner. "What have you got to lose?"

What indeed? The words were like a cold splash of water. What was she thinking? Sure, George might not know which class she attended, but Devon had eyes all over the gym. Word would surely get back to him. She had already broken enough rules today.

With a regretful shrug, she replied, "Next time."

"No problem." The young man gave her a farewell wave and bounded off into the room.

Sighing, Jane tossed her bag over one shoulder and continued the walk down the hall to the yoga room.

George had the car running and at the front entrance when she stepped out of the front door exactly an hour later. He cleared his throat meaningfully as she slid into the back seat. "We're behind schedule now. If we want to be home by three, we'll have to hurry."

Any tension that had been erased by the intense yoga stretches instantly resumed its position in her neck and shoulders.

They quickly finished the rest of her errands. Jane was especially pleased because the wine steward at their favorite store had just received a shipment of a special red blend they both felt Devon would love. She had adjusted her menu for the evening to accommodate the new wine and she was excited for her husband to come home and enjoy a luxurious meal. With any luck, the sumptuous meal would temper any lingering annoyance over being called twice, at least in one day.

After being dropped off by George, Jane, feeling a not-so-secret relief to finally be alone, dropped off the groceries in the kitchen and hung up the dry cleaning in the laundry room. Devon hated the way the dry cleaners mass-steamed his shirts and preferred she iron them by hand. She would tackle the ironing as soon as she got dinner started.

As she scrubbed the potatoes, the house phone rang again. Jane finished the potato, set it on a paper towel to dry, and picked up the receiver.

"Hello?"

"Hey, girl…" Sara's cheery voice filled the phone line.

"Oh, hi Sara," Jane greeted, clutching the phone between her ear and shoulder as she reached for another potato. She needed to get them in the oven to bake within the next ten minutes for them to be ready when dinner was served at 5:00. "What's up?"

"Paul just asked me to check on the menu for Saturday's dinner," Sara said apologetically.

Jane smiled to herself. More likely, Devon had hounded Paul about the menu until he agreed to call his wife. She rolled her eyes a little. She had never once, in her entire life, made a misstep on a dinner party menu. Her mother had taught her well. Still, Devon worried obsessively about any event that he hosted. Everything had to be perfect. Even though Paul and Sara were technically co-hosts for the dinner party on Saturday, Jane knew that ultimately, she would be responsible for overseeing all of the details. Devon didn't trust anyone else.

"I emailed the caterer some suggestions yesterday," she offered. "He's going to get me a sample menu by tomorrow."

"Of course, you have everything under control. Why did I even bother to call?" Sara laughed and then asked, "Seriously, though, do you want me to come over early to help you set up?"

Jane could just imagine the reaction Devon would have to Sara's presence in the house. She was a lovely woman, but her attention to detail left something to be desired.

"That is sweet of you to offer, but I think we have it all under control," she replied easily. And then, because she felt she owed Sara a little something, she added, "You can; however, sneak me in one of your famous brownies. I have a feeling I'll need the sugar rush." The statement was entirely untrue, but Jane knew it would make Sara feel more involved.

The timer on the oven went off just as she said her goodbyes. Jane set down the phone to check on the London broil roasting in the oven. The second oven was heating up, and she quickly wrapped her potatoes in foil and slid them in. Glancing at her watch, she mentally calculated the minutes remaining until 5:00. Just under an hour. She would put the salad together at the last minute so it would be crisp and cold. She uncorked the wine to let it breathe.

Reaching into the glass cabinets above the counter, she removed two china plates. They were an ornate blue and gold pattern that Jane personally felt was a bit overstated, but Devon loved the richness of the bold pattern and tonight Jane hoped that the elaborate table setting might distract Devon from any tensions lingering from earlier today. She set the table with a formal setting and added fresh flowers to the centerpiece. When it was complete, the table could have been featured in a magazine spread. Jane just had a knack for putting things together. And she had plenty of practice. With a smile of satisfaction, Jane moved upstairs to dress for dinner. She was cutting it short on time and wanted to be ready and relaxed when her husband walked in the door. Despite everything, she had had a successful day managing to get everything on Devon's list complete and squeezing in a yoga class.

She was looking forward to spending a quiet evening with her husband.

At 5:00, Jane, dressed in silk pants and a white top, glanced at the kitchen clock. The table was set. The steak had rested for ten minutes and was ready to slice. The salad was crisp and waiting for dressing and the wine was breathing on the counter. Her timing, as usual, had been impeccable. She smiled happily at her perfect kitchen scene and breathed a sigh of relief. Devon should walk in any minute, and everything was just right.

At 6:00, Jane tossed the salad into the trash can and reached into the fridge for lettuce and tomatoes. Salads were always tricky. If she left it in the fridge, it lost some of its natural aromas, but if she left it out at room temperature, the lettuce always started to wilt too soon. She had learned from her mother to always have extra salad makings – it was easier to start fresh than risk serving a wilted salad. She checked the meat, which she had covered with aluminum foil to keep the heat in. That was also a risky move. She would have to remember to remove the foil as soon as she heard the doorknob. Devon always liked to assume his dinner had come out of the oven precisely when he entered the house.

At 7:00, Jane stood staring into the refrigerator, wringing her hands. The London Broil was too cool to serve, and if she attempted to reheat it, it would almost certainly dry out. The potatoes, perfect two hours ago, were cold and hard. Dinner, as prepared at 5:00, was completely ruined.

Jane placed her index fingers on her temple, pressing slightly, as her mind worked through the ingredients left in her pantry. She didn't know if she had thirty minutes or two hours until Devon would be home. She had checked his schedule and did not see any notations that he would be late tonight. It wouldn't occur to him to call and let her know, and it would be unthinkable for her to call him and ask.

She had fresh salmon, the only seafood Devon tolerated, in the fridge. It wouldn't be his favorite, but it was quick and simple. She would steam some vegetables and throw together yet another salad. Jane quickly rinsed off the fish and patted it dry. She heated the oven and seasoned the salmon. Ten minutes later, the fish was baking and the vegetables were in the steamer. She had done it.

She rushed upstairs to change clothes. She smelled like the kitchen, which some men appreciated, but Devon liked her to smell like Chanel No. 5 at all times. And with her extensive wardrobe, she could afford to change clothes more than once.

Now wearing a flowered skirt and silk top, Jane wiped down the kitchen counters and took the trash to the receptacle outside the apartment, making sure any traces of the previous meal were nonexistent. She didn't want to make Devon feel bad for missing dinner. The salmon meal would be just fine. Well, except for the wine. She knew the red wine would be too heavy for the salmon, but she had little choice. She had already opened the bottle, and she didn't want it to go to waste.

At 8:00, Jane was pacing the kitchen floor, trying to determine a light meal that she could keep in the fridge. The salmon was disposed of outside next to the London Broil. The kitchen was void of any indications of previously prepared meals. Jane wasn't sure what step to take. Making a third hot meal, especially at this late hour, seemed like a waste. Still, she didn't want to make any assumptions. If Devon came home, at whatever time that might be, she wanted to have something prepared to serve him. There wasn't a question in her mind that she would wait up no matter how late he might be. It was her duty as his wife to make sure he was taken care of; no matter if it was an inconvenience or not. She had roasted chicken and could put together a salad if need be.

At 8:30, the front door opened, and Devon entered, setting his briefcase down on the hall table. Jane gave a quick glance around the kitchen. It was as spotless as it had been when she stepped foot in it this morning. When Devon didn't immediately inquire about dinner, Jane assumed that he had already eaten. A fleeting touch of relief glanced over her. She hadn't been sure of how the chicken salad would go over. Now, she wouldn't have to find out.

The wine had been transferred to a decanter and sat on the bar with the other liquor bottles. Jane quickly made her way over in that direction. "Would you like wine or something stronger?"

Devon walked past her towards the stairs. His manner seemed relaxed as he replied, "Wine would be great. I'm going to take a shower."

With the sound of the shower running upstairs, Jane took the lid off the crystal decanter and let the wine breathe for just a moment. She made a quick tour of the living room, adjusting a pillow and shifting a magazine on the coffee table. By the time Devon returned, his wine glass was positioned on the table next to his Eames chair, and she was sitting primly on the sofa across from him.

"Busy day today?" she asked with a smile.

Devon glanced in her direction. "It was fine," he commented, taking a sip of his wine. He paused for a moment, contemplating, and then said, "Not bad. A little heavy for this time of night."

But perfect for dinner at five o'clock, Jane thought, but kept her expression understanding and sympathetic. She had been hoping for a relaxing and easy evening to make up for all of the phone calls Devon had received on her behalf today. With any luck, his late evening had kept him preoccupied enough to forget about the earlier phone calls. It wouldn't hurt to have that discussion postponed as long as possible, as far as Jane was concerned.

She felt her stomach rumble a little and tucked her feet under her body to adjust her position. She, naturally, had been waiting to eat dinner with her husband, but making something for herself at this time would be rude. She'd have a larger breakfast in the morning.

Devon reached for the TV remote and switched on the cooking channel. He was obsessed with cooking shows. Jane could take them or leave them, but she watched diligently whenever they were on. It wasn't uncommon for Devon to make a note on his daily list, "Make that dinner from the show we saw the other night". It would be up to her to interpret correctly which meal he was referring to and prepare it exactly like it was portrayed on the show. It had become a little game to her, and she was getting fairly adept at predicting which preparations would come up for later discussions.

After the first show, Jane noticed Devon's wine glass had dipped below halfway. She rose from the sofa and reached for the wine decanter. Her husband wouldn't dream of getting up to refill his own glass. As she leaned over her husband to refill his glass, his hand suddenly shot out and grabbed her by the arm. "Gotcha," he said, his voice low and menacing. She jumped but managed to keep the crystal in her hands without spilling red wine all over the floor. He gave her a grin and removed his hand.

Heart pounding in apprehension, Jane quickly returned the wine and took her place on the sofa.

"Oh, by the way," Devon commented, turning to face her. His pupils were black. "Nice haircut."

Full panic set in. She raised her hand to her hair. He never, ever commented on her hair, unless something was wrong. She could tell he was not happy. Now, he was looking at her expectantly. She cleared her throat and said, "Thank you."

"You know–I wouldn't change a thing about it," he continued, staring at her hard before adding, "Something I would have told you–had you asked."

"I…," she started, but he held up his hand.

"It just makes my day complete when I am interrupted from my work, important work," he stressed, his voice sharp, "to answer questions about why my wife is disobeying my requests…"

"I didn't…"

"And then," he continued, interrupting her, "I come home from a long day and there is not even dinner on the table."

What? Jane stopped breathing for a moment. She had made not one, but three, dinners this evening. He hadn't even bothered to tell her what he had been doing all of these hours. He was working himself into a rage. Jane's heart filled with dread. She knew, without a doubt, that this conversation wasn't going to end well.

"What did you do all day?" he asked. "Yoga?" He said the word as if it were an expletive. "Is that how you spend all of your time these days?"

"Of course not," she started to explain. "Look," she pointed to the dining room. "I have the table set. I used your favorite china."

He stood up and switched off the TV. Deliberately, he walked into the dining room where the table showcased a full place setting for two people. He picked up one of the heavy china plates and examined it carefully. Jane held her breath as he turned it over in his hands. Then, without warning, he flung it in her direction. Startled, Jane barely moved out of the way before the dish hit the wall behind her and shattered. Before she could recover, he went plate by plate, throwing the dishes in her direction. Tiny pieces of ceramic nicked her legs where the plates hit the floor around her. Jane felt like a rag doll as she ducked and dodged flying dishware. She was afraid to run because she thought Devon might give chase. And if he caught her, that would be worse than getting hit by a dish. Much worse.

Once all of the plates had been destroyed, Devon turned to her with a malicious stare.

"You know," he scolded, "I expect my wife, who doesn't have to work thanks to the generous life I afford her, to take care of our home. I expect her to take care of me." He looked around in disgust. "Look at the mess you've made." He picked up a large shard of glass and examined it and then held it up, pointing it at her. "You know this sharp edge could have cut my hands." He held up his hand and moved it close to her face. "Hands that work all day to afford you this comfortable lifestyle. A lifestyle that you just have to disparage at every turn, don't you?"

His expression turned to a menacing scowl. "You've never appreciated what I do for you. The hours I put in. To give you all of this and, as a reward, you destroy the things I purchased?" As his fury mounted, his movements became unpredictable, and the shard wavered precariously close to her face. Jane held her breath and fought to remain perfectly still, afraid that he would nick her.

He kicked the pieces of China at his feet. "Clean up this mess. I'd better not see one spec of this trash on the floor when I wake up in the morning." He gave her a mocking smile and held up the shard in his hand. "I think I'll just hang on to this piece for a little while, just in case…"

Jane swallowed thickly at the implied threat, but merely nodded her head in response. As he started to walk away, he called over his shoulder. "Oh, and make it quick. I will be waiting for you upstairs. She knew what that meant. There wouldn't be making love this evening. There would only be punishment.

Jane knelt on the floor with a numb heart. Her body wanted to cry, but she had forgotten how long ago. Instead, she picked up several of the larger blue and gold pieces and held them together as if she could bring back the whole pattern. There were jagged edges and huge gaps where pieces were shattered or missing. She stared at the mangled pattern that had just moments ago been perfectly meshed. The once beautiful pattern looked broken and ugly. She dropped the pieces into the trash with a shudder. She knew what it felt like to be broken and ugly. It was such a shame to destroy something so beautiful for no reason at all.

And it was all her fault. If she had just stuck to Devon's plan. She had known all along that Devon would be upset that she hadn't just followed his directions. She hadn't cared in the moment, but now she wasn't certain that moment of freedom was worth it. He would be angry at her for a long time.

With a heavy heart, she scraped every piece of China into a dustpan, feeling the tiny pieces dig into her knees. With quick movements, she swept the floor and disposed of the trash. While she dreaded what lay ahead of her, she was keenly aware of Devon's parting words. Making him wait would only make things worse for her. She finished up in the kitchen and headed silently up the stairs. She accepted her fate and prayed for it to be over soon.

Devon looked pointedly at his watch as she entered the room.

She didn't want to look at Devon–to see the cruelty in his eyes, but she knew if she averted her eyes, it would just make things worse. She met his gaze. She kept her expression neutral despite the heavy pounding of her heart. She knew from experience if she allowed him to see her emotions, it would fuel his depravity. Sometimes, it just didn't matter.

He smiled at her–a deep, malicious smile that froze her to her very soul.

He caressed his hand down her pale cheek. "I have to be careful, don't I? I don't want to leave any marks on your delicate skin. We do have an important event on Saturday. And I know you'll want to look your best."

His tone sent a river of ice down her veins, but she did not move. He stared at her for a moment longer, his hand resting on her cheek. Then he raised it and slapped her. Not hard enough to leave a permanent mark, but she felt the sting, nonetheless.

She closed her eyes and moved into her own private inner world. It was a place where she could keep her heart safe. In her heart, she could not believe this was how a man and woman were supposed to interact–how could a man who professed to love her so much treat her body so callously? Despite everything, in her core, she had been trained to obey her husband, and this was what her husband wanted. She didn't have a say, no matter how she felt inside. This was the only life she had ever known. Not only did she not have the strength to fight back, but she also didn't have the experience to even question the situation. Instead, on nights like this, she allowed her mind to escape deep to a safe and protected place.

Later, as she lay bruised and sore in the bed, Devon slid out from beside her and reached for his robe. Usually, she felt lonely when he left; but, tonight, she sincerely hoped he wouldn't return until after she fell asleep. Hopefully, then, there would be less of a chance of a repeat performance.

Whatever it was Devon did in his office, she prayed it would take his mind off of punishing her.

Chapter Four

On Saturday, Jane slipped a dangling diamond earring through her earlobe as Devon emerged from the shower.

"Shouldn't you be downstairs overseeing the caterer?" he asked. His voice was clipped, but not in anger. After the previous incident, Devon had left her alone for the rest of the week, much to her relief. As always, Devon never mentioned the incident and, true to his word, not a mark marred her delicate skin. Well, at least the skin visible to anyone looking at her.

Devon's quick pacing of the bathroom belied his nervousness over the dinner. The Chief of Staff would be in attendance as well as most of the high-value contributors to the hospital. Devon insisted everything be perfect. Even more perfect than usual. Not only was it important to raise funds for the hospital, but bragging rights were at stake. The couple who hosted the party last year had raised an impressive sum for the hospital and Devon did not want to be second to anyone. Folks in Miami took their fundraising seriously and Devon wanted to ensure that his name was in the conversation for the next year.

She stood up from the dressing table and slipped on the ivory silk jacket that matched her pants. The light suit was offset by a rose-colored camisole and, together, the outfit was feminine and very flattering. It also covered the large bruises on her thighs and forearms.

"I'm on my way down, now," she replied calmly. She had used this caterer many times, and he was very familiar with the demands of the Rawlings couple.

Jane smiled with satisfaction as she descended the staircase. Below her, the living area was alight with soft candlelight. The full-length windows showed off the sparkling lights of the surrounding city. The dim ambiance showcased the golden hour perfectly. The large dining table in the formal dining room was set with Wedgewood china and centerpieces featuring white roses. In the background, soft jazz music was just audible.

She made her way into the kitchen, where the caterer was setting out the last of the appetizer platters to be passed by uniformed waiters as the guests arrived. Since the galley kitchen was open to the rest of the apartment, meal preparation was taking place in the large walk-in pantry just off the kitchen, which boasted a large island and plenty of room to prepare the plated dinners. She gave the caterer a kiss on both cheeks as he placed the final touches on the trays. All of his staff dressed in crisp maroon jackets with black pants. They were impeccably groomed and camouflaged to blend in with the background. The caterer had witnessed one of Devon's meltdowns years ago where he had belittled Jane in front of the wait staff. Since then, she had felt an inexplicit bond with the man that knew to do everything in his power to see that the food and drinks were nothing short of perfection. For Jane's sake–not Devon's.

The doorbell rang, and Jane observed as the greeter, also provided by the catering company, answered the door before a second chime could sound. Devon was certain to notice a detail like that.

Sara and Paul entered the room. The greeter took their coats and handed them a glass of wine as they entered the foyer. The music and candlelight guided them into the living room, where waiters with full trays of appetizers waited attentively. As soon as she saw both Sara and Paul content with a glass of wine and a stuffed fig appetizer, Jane allowed herself a small smile of satisfaction. It was the perfect trial run. And things had gone without a glitch.

Confident things were flowing smoothly, Jane, carrying a glass of water, entered the living room.

"Jane," Sara squealed, holding out her arms.

Jane kissed her friend on both cheeks and then did the same with Paul. It was a touch old-fashioned, she knew, but Jane had been raised with traditional manners and, to her, it still felt right.

"This room is simply amazing," Sara enthused. "The candles, the flowers… Everything is just perfect." She grinned impishly. "Would you come decorate my house?"

Paul put his arm around his wife and echoed teasingly, "Yes, please?"

Jane laughed. "I really didn't do much. The caterer did most of the work."

They all knew that statement wasn't remotely true, but it made Jane feel charitable to deflect the credit.

Guests arrived in force, and Jane found herself mingling and greeting the newcomers over the next half hour. While always the gracious hostess, she kept one eye on the appetizer and drink trays to ensure they were always completely full. It meant extra work for the staff to continue to refill the trays, but Devon liked things a certain way and it was just easier to make sure that happened.

She wasn't sure when he had appeared, but Jane spotted Devon from across the room and felt her heart skip a beat. He looked dashing in his black suit with this thick hair combed away from his face. He held a glass of wine and chatted with a group of men near the dining room. Jane had received so many compliments on the house and the service that she was feeling warm and happy inside. He must have felt her gaze on him because he turned his head and made eye contact with her. She gave him a loving smile, and he responded with a slight nod of the head.

A second later, he stood by her side. She gazed up at him in adoration, waiting for him to acknowledge her efforts at the party. Everyone was having a wonderful time. She had even overheard the Chief of Staff comment on how delicious the chicken wraps tasted.

He leaned over and whispered in her ear, "White roses?"

Taken aback, Jane blinked and said stupidly, "What?"

Devon grabbed her arm, his fingers pressing so deeply into her skin she felt pressure down to the bone, and pulled her away from the crowd of guests. Keeping his face perfectly pleasant, he questioned in an icy whisper, "Where did you get the roses? The local grocery store?"

Jane cringed internally. She closed her eyes and took a deep breath as bruising jolts shot down her arm from his tight grip. She wouldn't be able to respond without a grimace until she inwardly controlled the pain. The hesitation gave her a brief moment to compose an appropriate answer. She couldn't believe she made such an obvious mistake in the choice of flowers. Naturally, Devon would hate the idea of having anything as ordinary as roses. It didn't matter that the arrangements were tastefully arranged and perfect for the décor. Anyone could have white roses at their party.

No, they had to be special. Something no one else could have acquired. A mistake like this could ruin the rest of the evening. Devon's grip on her arm had not loosened, and her arm was tingling with numbness. Panic rose in Jane's throat; but she held it back. She couldn't let that happen. Not right now, anyway.

Thinking on her feet, Jane smiled back at him and managed not to show any sign of her physical discomfort. "Of course not. These were flown in from France. They're very rare. And very expensive. But they look lovely on the table, don't you think? I didn't think you would mind the extra cost…"

Devon held her gaze sharply, trying to see if she would flinch, but Jane held her ground. Sure, the entire statement was a lie, but she doubted seriously Devon would check. He tested her ability to stay composed.

To her relief, the Chief of Staff and his wife chose that moment to approach the couple. Devon released her arm, and Jane resisted the urge to reach over to rub out the numbness. Instead, she smiled at the couple." It's so nice to see you again."

After air kisses all around, the chief's wife said loudly, "I simply love the centerpieces. They are so elegant."

"Thank you," Jane replied simply, daring to cast a sideways glance at her husband.

"The roses were imported from France, you know,"

Devon interjected, ignoring her. With a charming smile, he placed one hand on his bosses' shoulder and the other on his wife's shoulder before leading the couple toward the bar. "Probably cost me a fortune…" she heard him say with a smug laugh as he walked off.

Jane allowed herself to release a sigh of relief as her husband's voice faded into the distance. She was happy to have escaped the confrontation relatively unscathed. Alone for a moment, she lifted her hand to gently massage the arm where Devon's grip had been. It was already sore and bruising beneath the delicate silk fabric of her jacket.

"Is everything okay?"

Startled, Jane turned to see Sara standing next to her. She hadn't heard her friend approach. She dropped her hand immediately. "Of course." She knew her voice sounded a pitch too high and even somewhat shaky, so she stopped and took a breath to reclaim her carefully modulated tone. "Why wouldn't it be?"

Sara kept her gaze focused on her friend. "No reason. It just looked like you and Devon were having a mighty intense conversation."

Jane forced a laugh. "You know Devon. He likes everything to be perfect."

"What's not perfect?" Sara asked incredulously.

Jane shook her head. "No, everything is perfect. He was just asking where the roses came from." She rolled her eyes and pretended to sound ashamed. "I might have forgotten to tell him I had them flown in from France." She had already started the lie, might as well see it all the way through.

Sara laughed, obviously relieved, "France, really?"

Jane just shrugged and smiled. She certainly hoped

somehow France was known for its white roses. She had a feeling there might be a run on them for future local parties.

Sara reached out and took Jane's arm. "You would let me know if anything was wrong, wouldn't you?"

Jane bit the inside of her bottom lip as her friend's fingers pressed into the wounded flesh on her arm, but outwardly nodded and smiled. "Of course I would. But everything is fine. I think everyone is having a good time, don't you?"

Now Sara nodded enthusiastically. "Everyone is having a wonderful time."

"Good," Jane whispered the word under her breath as her friend moved off. She preferred to be an excellent hostess and remain on the sidelines. She spent the rest of the evening making the guests feel welcome and ensuring everyone had what they needed.

Dinner was a success. Each course was timed perfectly and the food was fresh and delicious. For once, even Devon had trouble finding things to complain about.

When the last guest departed, Devon took his scotch into his office to wind down while Jane oversaw the caterer and staff as they packed up and a cleaning crew came through to perform a final clean. It was almost midnight, but Devon wouldn't dream of going to bed without the house being spotless. In the past, that duty had been left to Jane, who might not get to bed until the early hours of the morning, but she had secretly worked out a deal with the caterer to supply a cleaning staff as part of the normal catering service. Devon didn't pay attention to details like that and had said nothing when the bill arrived, so Jane kept the service. While she still had to stay up to supervise, four or five people could quickly take care of what would take Jane the rest of the evening. Naturally, she would have to go through and do a final clean after they left to get things up to Devon's standards, but it was worth every penny to Jane.

At 2:00 AM, Jane fell into bed beside her husband. He snored softly, a trait most likely induced by the amount of hard liquor consumed that night, and he didn't stir when she slid in beside him. She waited for a moment, holding her breath, in case Devon was merely playing a game with her, but after several moments, he rolled over onto his side and continued sleeping soundly. Jane released a small sigh of relief and allowed her head to relax against the pillow. Not waiting up for her showed he had been pleased with the evening, making Jane's life a whole lot easier.

The next morning, Jane awoke alone in the bed. She glanced at the nightstand clock. It was only 7:00 AM. She hadn't heard the alarm go off and had not awoken when Devon got up, so she had no idea what time he had left the room.

Wrapping a silk robe around her, she quickly brushed her hair and washed her face. She went downstairs to see if Devon had left a note for her. The downstairs was quiet. The kitchen was dark and deserted–no sign of any disturbance and no note on the counter. Had Devon left for work already? Jane stopped in front of the door to his office. She didn't hear any sounds from inside but didn't want to start her day with the risk of upsetting Devon if he were in his office.

Biting her lip, Jane peered beneath the door frame. From her vantage point, the room looked dark.

Still, to be safe, Jane took her time upstairs dressing.

She gathered the laundry from the hampers in the bathroom and then crossed over into the bedroom. She thought today would be a good day to change out the sheets and pillowcases. Dropping her bundle beside the bed, she leaned over to start removing the pillowcases. As the dirty clothes hit the floor something hard smacked against her bare foot.

"Ouch," she grumbled reaching down to move the pile of clothes. When she picked up Devon's suit pants, his cell phone tumbled out onto the floor.

Jane snapped upright. She bit her lip and stared at the electronic device as if it were a snake. Devon never, ever, left his phone unattended. Normally, he left his phone in his office where she was strictly forbidden to enter, and she thought little of it; but, now, with it lying there in front of her, Jane had the overwhelming urge to pick it up.

Devon would most certainly not approve. He was fiercely private to the point where he left the room every time the phone rang in her presence.

Jane leaned over and picked up the phone, holding it in her hand. Her heart pounded inside her chest, and she felt certain any second Devon would come bursting through the door demanding she drop the phone.

Just the thought was enough to give Jane pause. She actually wasn't 100% certain Devon wasn't coming up the staircase right this very moment. If he had any inclination that she had access to his private phone, he would not be pleased. She slid the phone back into the pants pockets and lay them across the side chair in the room along with his jacket, as if she were preparing to take them to the dry cleaners. That way if Devon came home and noticed they had been moved, she could just claim she hadn't checked the pockets. There was nothing for her to worry about at this time.

She stripped the bed and gathered the remaining laundry items, hurrying down the stairs. For the rest of the morning, she busied herself with the laundry, reorganizing the pantry and a number of other meaningless chores. But, in her mind, the picture of that phone remained a constant presence. It was the ultimate forbidden fruit.

Under the pretext of taking the trash down to the garbage shoot, Jane detoured through the parking garage. Her Mercedes sat untouched in its space. The space next to hers was empty.

Devon's car was gone.

Dumping the trash bag into the bin, Jane hurried back upstairs and locked the door. Then she went around to the front door and made sure it was locked as well. With her heart racing so loudly she could feel the pulse in her ears, Jane crossed through the living room and stood in front of the door to Devon's office. She placed her hand on the knob and closed her eyes. She had never once, in all the time they lived here, been alone in Devon's office. Occasionally, he invited her in to show her something on the computer or in the newspaper he was reading, but, never, ever would she dream of invading his private space without his permission.

Until now.

What if he was in there – waiting for her to make a mistake?

But he wasn't

His car was gone.

He wasn't home.

Was he?

With agonizing slowness, she turned the knob.

It was locked.

Of course, it was locked. Jane dropped her head forward, exhaling. Devon always locked the door when he left.

And his car was gone.

Devon was not in the house.

This was not a setup.

He had merely forgotten his phone.

Giving up all pretense of unconcern, Jane ran up the stairs into the bedroom. Devon's pants and jacket lay just where she had left them.

She reached into the pocket and pulled out the phone. It was one of those new models–sleek and shiny. She ran her finger lightly over the case. If she exerted any pressure, the screen would light up.

Jane bit her lip. What harm would it do if she just touched the screen? Certainly, the phone was password protected. All she could see was the screen saver. Maybe Devon kept a picture of her on his phone. Wouldn't that be a sweet gesture? She was kidding herself. He most likely had a picture of himself.

Jane pushed. The screen was a generic blue background. There were several icons floating on the screen with the familiar lock symbol front and center.

It was locked. Just as well…

Jane started to put the phone back and then stopped, her mind working with a feverous pitch. If she were Devon, what password would she use?

No. Just put it back.

Jane stared at the phone in her hand. Would he use her birthday?

The thought made her utter a short laugh aloud. He

probably didn't even know her birthday. George handled things like that for him.

Would he use his own birthday?

Now that was more like it.

Put it back.

Jane ran her finger over the lock icon. The password prompt filled the screen. Before she could talk herself out of it, Jane punched in the numbers. Surely, Devon wouldn't keep a password that simple.

When the lock disappeared from the screen, Jane actually let out a gasp of surprise. What was Devon thinking? Obviously, he was thinking no one but himself would have access to his private phone.

But now she did.

Jane sat down on the edge of the bed.

What was she doing? This was her husband's phone. His private property. She should just put it back where she found it and never think about it again.

Jane pushed the green talk button on the phone.

A list of recent calls appeared on the screen.

The last call had been made at 10:15 last night.

Jane frowned. That was right in the middle of the dinner party. Who was Devon calling at that time? She tried to remember if Devon had left the room for any extended time, but she had been so busy taking care of the guests she couldn't remember any specific events that stood out. Devon had been happy and relaxed for most of the evening as far as she was aware. Clearly, it was a business call that Devon had felt it necessary to make.

In the middle of his dinner party. Where most of his work colleagues were in attendance.

A call that had lasted… Jane checked the screen.

Nine minutes.

Jane ran her finger over the screen. All she had to do was push the button, and she would know.

Jane dropped the phone on the bed and stood up. Was she crazy? This was Devon's phone. What difference did it make who he was calling? It was none of her business. She was NOT going to give this another thought. And she was certainly NOT going to press the call button.

Across the room, the phone pulled at her like a magnet. Jane shook her head and turned her back to the bed. Even if she wanted to, he would know if she made a call on it. It would show up on the call history if he checked.

She paced the room, wringing her hands together, playing devil's advocate to her own mind. Why would he check his call history? He wouldn't have any reason to unless he was suspicious.

No. Jane shook her head and walked into the bathroom. She had no business invading Devon's personal space. It was inappropriate.

Reaching underneath the sink for the cleaning wipes, Jane began cleaning the already spotless countertops. As she moved her hand in a rhythmic circle, she leaned her head back to peer into the bedroom. The phone lay shamelessly winking at her from the bed.

Come and get me.

Jane stopped mid swirl.

What if Devon came home early to look for it?

That was not an unreasonable assumption. Devon hated being without his phone. If he found the phone lying on the bed, he would jump to conclusions even if Jane hadn't done anything wrong.

Jane dropped the rag and hurried back to the bed, picking up the phone and reaching for Devon's suit pants. She would just put everything back where it was in the first place and forget any of this had ever happened.

Even as the thought formed in her brain, Jane touched the screen for recent calls again. This time she pressed send before she could even formulate an argument against it. Before she could even react, she could hear the ringing of another phone across the line.

Dear God. What had she done?

The phone rang again. Jane's fingers hovered over the buttons, knowing she had gone too far.

On the third ring, she heard a click.

It was too late to turn back now.

With shaky hands, Jane lifted the phone to her ear. "Hello?"

It was a woman's voice, slightly breathless, as if she had hurried to reach the phone.

Jane stood paralyzed at the foot of the bed. The world around her started to move in slow motion. She held the phone to her ear, unmoving.

"Devon? Is that you?"

The woman's voice sounded soft and seductive. It didn't sound like the voice of a fellow colleague or insurance salesman or some other random call. It was an intimate voice. Someone who knew Devon. Someone who knew him well.

Jane pressed END.

She sat down on the edge of the bed before her knees could buckle beneath her. Her body felt tingly and numb at the same time. She knew her world had irrevocably changed, but she wasn't able to fully process the implications.

Without stopping to consciously think about it, Jane went to her dressing table and removed a notecard and pen from her top drawer. She copied the number with deliberate care from the phone and then placed the folded paper underneath the stack of notecards where it was not even remotely visible. She then took the phone and, just to be safe, wiped it down with a towel and placed it back inside Devon's pants pockets. She lay the pants and jacket back in the dry-cleaning bin precisely as she had found them this morning. She would rather risk the wrath of not having promptly taken in the dry cleaning than give the slightest indication that she knew he had forgotten his phone.

Jane spent the rest of the day moving about the house like a zombie. She cleaned and dusted, laundered and folded clothes, prepared dinner. All of the normal chores that made up her typical daily routine. But nothing felt routine anymore.

At five o'clock on the nose, the front door opened, and Devon entered the house. Jane felt her heart start to race inside her chest. The anxiety she had built up throughout the day threatened to explode, but Jane was an expert at hiding her feelings. She looked up from the salad she was tossing and said, "Hi Honey."

"Hey," Devon smiled at her and tossed his briefcase next to the hallway table. "Dinner ready?"

"It is," Jane said, her voice calm and polite. "Your wine glass is on the table."

The table was set with the everyday china, but Jane had rearranged some roses from last night into a lovely centerpiece. She knew Devon would appreciate it since those roses were now considered "special."

He touched one of the petals and sat down at one end of the table. Jane served up the roasted chicken, fresh out of the oven and crisp grilled asparagus along with the salad she had just finished tossing. She paired the meal with a crisp white wine. Devon was relaxed during dinner, and Jane didn't sense any tension in the air. She ate her meal while he chatted about sports and the weather. Luckily, Jane wasn't expected to participate much because her head was spinning with conflicting emotions. On one hand, she was terrified he would know she had used his phone and on the other hand, that voice kept playing in a loop in her mind. "Devon, is that you?" Who was it? And how did she know her husband?

After dinner, Devon switched from wine to scotch and moved to the other room. Jane stayed in the kitchen, drying off his wine glass to put back in the cabinet. She took her time, savoring the peaceful silence.

Devon called out from the sofa where he was watching the sports channel. "Did you come across my phone today?"

The glass trembled in her hands, and she quickly pushed it into place and shut the cabinet door. She made a pretense of wiping her hands on the dishtowel while taking several calming breaths. Finally, she replied, "No. Is it in your office?"

"I wouldn't have asked you if it was in my office, now would I?" Devon snarkily retorted.

"No, I guess not," Jane said, still puttering in the kitchen. She was desperately afraid if Devon looked her in the face, he would see the lie written all over it. She was normally a master at hiding her emotions; but this event had shaken her to her very core. "In any case, I haven't seen it."

She was met with silence. Jane didn't know if that was a good thing or a bad thing. She didn't dare leave the kitchen to find out. Instead, she opened the refrigerator and began rearranging jars lined up on the side shelf.

"I'm going to take a shower," Devon announced a few moments later and went upstairs.

Jane breathed a sigh of relief. She spent another thirty minutes rearranging the immaculate kitchen and then made her way up the stairs. She expected to find Devon in bed, reading the newspaper or working on his laptop. She did not expect to run into him, fully dressed, coming down the stairs.

She paused on the staircase. With a consorted effort, she affected a casual pose and asked nonchalantly, "Are you going somewhere?"

Her husband gave her a dismissive glance as he brushed past her and made his way downstairs. "I have some errands to run."

She glanced at her watch. At almost ten o'clock at night? An alarm went off in her brain, but she held her tongue, knowing it was better to be silent. He wore casual pants and a button-down shirt. He could easily be going to the grocery store or the local big box store – both were open well past this hour. That made perfect sense.

Except Devon didn't do those things.

Ever.

A full five minutes after the front door slammed shut, Jane made her way into the bedroom. Barely daring to breathe, she stepped inside Devon's closet and checked the hamper. His suit jacket and pants were there inside where they had been all day.

She picked the pants up gingerly, her heart racing in anticipation.

The pockets were empty.

Chapter Five

Stephanie stood up from the sofa to refill her glass of wine as the opening strains of her favorite dancing competition came on the TV. She knew full well that it was silly, mindless TV, but she enjoyed the escape.

It was just after ten o'clock. She hadn't heard from Devon yet, but she had her phone with her and wasn't worried about the time. She had gone for a long run earlier in the evening to wash away the tension from work. The past week had been less chaotic with the large deal they closed last week, but Stephanie had several new projects ramping up and her days were always busy. Brad Jensen had stopped by the day after the happy hour, complaining good-naturedly of a hangover and expressing his disappointment that she hadn't been able to make it back to the bar. He was open and friendly, and she thought that they could be friends–if Devon allowed her to have friends, that was. To be on the safe side, she had been sociable, but not encouraging. Still, it felt like over the past week, Brad had turned up in the hallway or the coffee bar every time she walked by. Or maybe she was just noticing him more often.

At 10:15, the sound of a car pulling into her driveway caught her attention. She went to the window and glanced through the blinds. It was Devon's Mercedes.

Surprised, Stephanie pushed thoughts of Brad from

her mind and dashed into the bathroom. Though she had showered after her run, her hair was a mess. She pulled her still damp hair into a loose ponytail. She had on soft casual pants and a T-shirt, which would have to do. At least she wore nothing underneath, which Devon would most certainly appreciate.

She headed for the kitchen to grab a second wine glass. Devon rarely visited her late at night, preferring mostly to stop by on the way to or from work, but she was would never turn him away.

For a fleeting second, she thought of the call she had received earlier in the day. It had come from Devon's phone. There was no question about that. But no one had spoken. That was the part that kept nagging at her conscious. It would be easy to say that the call had been inadvertent, but Stephanie knew better. It wouldn't be like Devon to accidentally hit the send button, either. He was very precise about his actions. No, she had a feeling someone else had made that call. Someone who didn't want to reveal his or her identity. She did not plan to mention the incident to Devon, but she wondered if he would bring it up.

By the time he reached her front door, Stephanie waited with a fresh glass of wine for him.

"Hey, you," he whispered, taking the glass from her hands and pulling her into his arms.

"Hey, yourself," she replied, allowing her body to melt into his. "This is a nice surprise."

"I missed you," he growled, nuzzling her neck.

He smelled of soap and clean aftershave. For as strong as she was professionally, Stephanie loved the feeling of protection being in Devon's arms gave her – even if she knew it was only temporary.

Devon set down his glass and led Stephanie back to her bedroom. His hands were strong and steady as he removed her clothing, pausing to smile when the removal of her pants revealed nothing but bare skin. He lay her back onto the bed and spread her legs before him.

She started to reach for him, but he yanked her wrists together and pinned her hands over hear head. His grip was tight. Very tight.

"Hey," she called out, wriggling her hands against his.

"I didn't love what you did this morning," he said, pinning her beneath him.

"What are you talking about?" she asked, genuinely confused.

"You had an orgasm without me. I want to be the one to make you come."

He stared into her eyes. His eyes were dark and dangerous.

"Okay." She was still confused. He had seemed fine this morning. She had no idea he'd been upset. "It was no big deal…"

"It was a big deal to me."

She felt a tremor of fear trickle down her spine at the venom in his voice. His grip on her hands tightened even more. Devon had never been rough with her before, and she wasn't at all interested in starting now. She struggled against him again, trying to break free, but he held her in a firm grip, staring at her with flaming eyes.

"Devon," she started, not liking the plaintive whine in her voice.

"Hush," he said, cutting her off, placing a finger to her lips. "I'm in control now."

Before she realized what was happening, Devon bit

her nipple. Hard. In her current state of disbelief, she was not ready for him and felt herself tear up at his roughness. His hold on her was so tight that she was unable to protect herself against his strength. She felt powerless and vulnerable.

They had sex and, with each thoughtless thrust, she felt her self-worth melt. This was not how people in love treated each other. This was not how she deserved to be treated. This was not how anyone deserved to be treated.

Her body tensed up. He ignored how she felt about what he was doing . Devon did not ask what she wanted. He squeezed her breast so hard, she gasped. But he ignored her pain.

She was fully clothed from the waist up and felt exposed and vulnerable, something she never experienced before.

His phone buzzed. He snapped out of his mindset and glanced away. Phone calls and messages popped in when he was on call.

"I have to get that," he said, as if he needed an excuse to stop what he was doing to her without permission.

The instant he released her hands, she scrambled off the bed. She grabbed her pants and began jamming her legs inside, using her clothing as an armor against the humiliation.

He mumbled in the distance. When he returned, she glared at him from across the room.

Devon sat at the edge of the bed as if he didn't have a care in the world. "Everything okay?"

The casual, non-concern in his voice sent Stephanie over the edge. "No," she said incredulously, "everything is not okay."

She held out her wrists, which were red and chafed from his grip. "This is not okay."

Devon reached out to her, his face transformed into one of concern. "I'm so sorry. I thought you would like that." His voice sounded sincere and full of concern, but something in his eyes glimmered with power.

Stephanie turned away from him, rubbing her wrists. "What on earth would make you think that?"

Devon had the grace to blush. "I read that bestselling book everyone was talking about. I thought that was what women wanted."

She turned back to him. "You don't need a book to tell you what I want. You know me." She pointed to her own chest. "You know who I am." Tears budded, but she held them in check. "At least I thought you did after three years together."

Devon scrambled off the bed, taking her in his arms and cradling her against his chest. "I'm sorry. I'm so sorry. I made a mistake. It won't ever happen again."

Still numb from the experience, she wanted more than anything to believe him. His hug was tight and secure. Stephanie allowed herself to be comforted because the minutes were fleeting. Before long, he would be tugged to get up and leave her. His warmth and smell replaced the balance that had just been so greatly upset.

He stroked her hair and said, "You know I left my phone at home today."

"What?" she asked. Then she was reminded of the strange call earlier.

"My phone. I didn't have it with me all day." After a second, he added, "You didn't try to call me, did you?"

Stephanie loosened the embrace and turned her head to look at him. He had no reason to ask her that. She never called him directly. Not even in an emergency. It was an unspoken rule between them. And, even if she broke the rule, her number would have shown up on his phone as a missed call. His questioning felt like an interrogation.

"Why would I call you?" Stephanie asked, keeping her expression neutral.

Devon held her gaze for a long moment and then said, "I'm sure you wouldn't." His eyes darkened just a bit. "You know better."

Stephanie sat up all the way. She was not impressed by the tone of his voice and was, in this moment, not interested in the direction the conversation was taking. She didn't need to be told what to do by anyone. She slipped out of bed and reached for her robe, turning her back to him. "I'm not sure what you mean by that; but if you are implying that I don't have any reason to call you during the day, then, yes, I know you are at work. I'm at work, too."

Her voice was curt, not only because she was stung by the implication of his words, but also because her feelings were hurt. She was always very careful to maintain her place in his life. She wouldn't dream of causing him the slightest inconvenience. For him to dismiss her so abruptly after everything she did for him – it did sting.

Devon sighed and reached out, grabbing the hem of her robe. "Come back here." His tone softened. "Let's not fight. I only have a few more minutes." He tugged harder on her robe, caressing her with those amazing eyes.

Reluctantly, she sat down on the edge of the bed, but she wasn't ready to let the subject drop. She turned to him and said sincerely, "You know, I'm not a threat to your marriage. I would never do anything to hurt you."

"I know," he said, wrapping his arms around her waist and pulling her to him. "You are amazing, and I love you so much."

I love you so much. Those were words he used freely with her. As he trailed kisses along the base of her neck, moving aside the robe she had just tied, she couldn't help but wonder if he was that vocal with his wife. Did he "love her so much", too? She told herself she didn't care. That the time he spent with her was enough, but sometimes she really wondered. He came to her home every day hungry for her, passionate for her, like a man starving.

For the first time in a long time, she wondered about his home life.

"Where does your wife think you are right now?"

Devon stopped what he was doing abruptly and stared at her. "What did you say?"

Stephanie didn't back down. She was always such a good mistress or whatever label people put on women in her position these days. Never asking any questions. Never complaining. Well, this time, she wanted an answer. "I asked, 'where does your wife…' "

"I heard what you asked." Devon cut her off. "I'm curious as to why you care."

"Because I'm entitled to know." Stephanie met his gaze, waiting for an answer. "What difference does it make why?"

He studied her for a moment, trying to read her face. Stephanie decided to pretend this was a business negotiation. She didn't want to give an inch. She wanted, no, she needed, to stand her ground.

They held gazes at a stale mate for what seemed like an eternity. Devon's jawline tensed for a split second and then, just as suddenly, as if he reached a decision, Devon's face softened. He reached out his hand to caress her cheek. "Exactly. What difference does it make why? I'm here with you and that's all that matters."

"I see." Stephanie knew she had lost the battle. He wasn't going to answer her. He never did. She stood up from the bed and went to get dressed, knowing the hour was getting late.

This time, Devon didn't try to convince her to stay. He got up and dressed as well, but he offered some parting words. "You know my wife would be devastated if I left her. She's very fragile. And she's accustomed to a certain lifestyle. She doesn't know anything different."

Devon's back was to her as he buttoned his shirt in the mirror. He spoke so matter of factly, as if her own feelings weren't a part of the equation.

Stephanie felt her heart break just a little as she listened to the words she had heard so many times. Devon took such efforts to protect the wife he claimed to care so little about. And now, in the middle of the night, he would rather leave Stephanie alone, broken hearted than risk upsetting his fragile wife.

A woman who needed him.

And couldn't live without him.

Tying her robe tightly around her waist, Stephanie followed Devon through the living room. At the front door, Devon turned and took her in his arms, pulling her to him. Despite everything, just the simple embrace made Stephanie's heart race. She wanted so much to be loved and protected and, when he was here, Devon provided that affection and security. Even if it was under false pretenses.

He lifted her face and kissed her, soft as a feather, on the lips. His voice was deep and sexy as he whispered, "Don't be sad, my love. I'll be back soon."

The smile she gave him wavered just a little.

Devon caressed her cheek. "You make me so happy, you know."

She nodded. Devon always told her that being with her took away the stress of his life, and she believed that. Now that he had gotten what he came for, Devon seemed content and relaxed. Stephanie's heart felt heavy as he walked out the door. As usual, he would take all of that happiness home to share with someone else.

Stephanie lay her head against the cool glass of her living room window and watched Devon slid into the driver's seat of his Mercedes.

What about her?

Didn't she deserve a little happiness?

Didn't she deserve something?

As she watched the taillights of Devon's car disappear into the darkness, Stephanie finally allowed the tears to pour like rain.

Chapter Six

Jane had spent the last two weeks moving around like a zombie. She completed her errands, performed the usual chores, even continued her yoga classes. But inside, she was completely numb. She stood in the kitchen in her silk nightgown with matching robe, waiting for the coffeemaker to chime so that she could fill her husband's travel mug with coffee. Holding the emerald green dishrag in her hand, she absently rubbed an imaginary speck from the countertop as she waited, but her mind was elsewhere.

For days, her thoughts had constantly floated back to the phone call and the woman's voice. It was imbedded in her brain like a virus. At least several times a day, she stood in front of her dresser holding the piece of paper hidden in her stationary box, staring at the numbers written there.

Who was this woman? What did she look like? How old was she?

And why was her husband calling her?

"Jane."

Devon's voice snapped her out of her reverie just as the coffee maker chimed. Draping the dishtowel neatly over the sink ledge, Jane quickly poured the coffee into Devon's travel mug, tightened the belt on her robe, and stepped out of the kitchen just as Devon crossed the living room toward the foyer. She pasted a smile on her face and said, "Here is your coffee for the trip into the office."

Devon took the mug from her hand and gave her a kiss on the forehead. "Thanks, babe."

She leaned into him like a flower reaching for the sun. Any show of affection, no matter how brief, brightened her spirits. She touched her husband's forearm with a soft caress. "Is there anything that you need me to pick up today?"

Devon stopped. "You could get some new towels for the bathroom. The ones we have are disgusting."

Jane sighed inwardly. The bathroom towels were brand new. She had washed them and put them out last week. Any brightness in Jane's eyes dimmed.

She handed him his briefcase, but did not make further eye contact. Devon didn't notice as he continued, "They're a terrible color, by the way. Looks like vomit."

They were sage green–a color he had specifically requested. But he was on a roll now. As he turned to the front door, he gestured toward the accent table in the front entrance. "And get some fresh flowers. Those are starting to wilt."

They weren't, but Jane caught the warning in his voice.

"I'll take care of everything," she assured him in an appeasing voice.

Devon paused again, his hand on the doorknob. "Don't spend too much time out shopping. This house is a wreck. Must I remind you that we have people coming over on Friday?"

As the door shut behind her husband, Jane sighed again and moved with heavy feet upstairs to her room to get dressed. She could never win that argument.

The house was spotless, but she would clean it from top to bottom in the afternoon. And whichever vase she forgot to put back perfectly in place, or whichever speck, imaginary or not, she forgot to dust would be noticed, and commented on, by her husband this evening. It was the story of her life.

But, first, a trip to the mall for towels.

As she dressed, Jane realized that since the towels were a last-minute discussion, Devon had not rung for George to drive her. A slow smile spread across her face. Devon had specifically said to pick up towels today, and she was certainly not authorized to have direct contact with George, the man worked for Devon, not her.

She didn't have a list.

Or a driver.

With a renewed spark to her step, Jane put on a pair of dark blue pants and a soft silk shirt. She threw on her makeup and the requisite jewelry and practically sprinted down the stairs into the kitchen. The keys to her Mercedes hung on the key rack next to the pantry. They had never been hidden or removed. It was her car, registered in her name, and she was certainly free to drive it–though she rarely did. It barely had 5,000 miles on it and still had a new car smell, but Devon always had something negative to say when she took it out. He made sure to point out a speck of dirt on the bumper or brake dust on the wheels. Or there would be a lengthy speech about women drivers and the dangers of being on the road. Over the years, it had simply become too much trouble. And besides, on most days, George was around.

But not today. Today, Jane was driving herself to the mall.

Safely ensconced in the soft leather seats of her car,

Jane started the engine and felt the soft purr of its power. The dashboard lights felt like an airplane control panel. She turned on the radio and the soft jazz station filled the car with its gentle beat. But Jane wasn't feeling particularly gentle. She turned the knob until she found a pop station with a young, hip beat that made the car vibrate.

Much more like it.

Part of her wanted to just sit and enjoy the moment, but the truth of the matter was that she needed to get her errands run. No matter how much fun the trip to the mall alone promised to be, she still had a house to clean before her husband returned.

As she nosed the Mercedes out of the parking garage onto the street, Jane was assailed by the sense of freedom. No one was watching her, or judging her, or reporting back to her husband. It felt amazing.

A cloudless blue sky surrounded her, and the sun filled the car with light as she hopped onto the South Dixy Highway and headed south. She knew exactly where she was headed. Dadeland Mall. It wasn't the closest shopping center, but it housed the largest Macys in Florida. And it was far enough away that she was unlikely to run into anyone that she, or her husband, knew.

With a smile, Jane reached into her bag and pulled out a pair of oversized sunglasses to slip on her nose. She felt exhilarated as she pressed her foot against the gas pedal, feeling the power of the luxury car as it rose to the speed limit.

As the city grew smaller in her rearview mirror, Jane's sense of independence increased. She allowed herself to imagine, for a brief moment, a life where she could simply enjoy being out in the open, feeling the rush of the city as it lived around her. Being a part of it on her own without the mandate of her husband. Where she could just make her own decisions.

The mall was bright and modern. At this time of the morning, Jane found herself surrounded by the moms pushing baby strollers and retired ladies in sneakers and khaki shorts power walking the levels of the mall. There was an energy surrounding her that felt exhilarating. Jane wore a huge smile as she strode through the giant Macy's anchoring the mall. It felt good to be independent without George lurking over her shoulder. She could relax and admire the beautiful displays lining the massive shelves. Well, to a certain extent.

"Can I help you?" The salesgirl was about her age, and greeted her with a friendly smile. Her name tag read, 'Rachel.'

For a second, Jane pretended like they were friends.

"Hi Rachel. I need the perfect green towels."

Lined on the shelves before her was every shade of green imaginable.

"Hmmm…" Rachel tapped her finger to her chin as she contemplated the selection.

Jane surreptitiously studied the woman standing next to her. She wore dark jeans and a flowing shirt. She was thin and tall and the jeans made her legs look long and lean. Her hair was cut short in a dark pixie highlighting the angular features of her face. In short, she looked young and fashionable without being too showy. How Jane wished she could just put on a pair of jeans to run errands. She wished she had a cute pixie cut instead of the same bob she'd had for years. She wished she could dress more her age. Instead of looking like a young, vibrant lady, Jane's outfit showed a woman much older than her years.

"How about this one?" Rachel held up a towel.

Jane tilted her head. "Does it look like vomit to you?"

Rachel burst into laughter. "I guess it does a little, now that you mention it."

Jane felt a little rush of pleasure at making the other woman laugh. "Well, that won't do."

For another ten minutes, the two women sorted through the different shades of green and finally settled on a jade green that each was convinced did not resemble vomit in any way. Jane bought a set of four towels and, as she was leaving, said with a warm smile, "Thank you, Rachel, for your help. I think these will be perfect."

Rachel smiled back. "You're welcome. It was fun. Good luck with those."

Feeling happy with her purchase, Jane strolled through the mall, looking in the store windows. She had to get going soon to keep on schedule, but she wanted to hang onto her independence for just a little while longer.

"Can I interest you in a new cell phone?"

Jane glanced at the young man with the long dreadlocks sitting on the stool outside of a kiosk representing one of the large cell phone providers.

She smiled, shook her head, and kept walking.

"No contract required," the kid called out as she moved past.

The words floated by her like a whispering wind.

Jane stopped and turned back. "What do you mean?"

Sensing an opportunity, the young man jumped off his stool and took several steps towards Jane. She did not move. He smiled, placed his hands on her shoulders and guided her back to the kiosk. "I mean - you don't have to sign anything. These are prepaid phones."

He watched her for a reaction and seeing none, quickly grabbed a phone from the rack and handed it to her. "You just put money in the account and when the minutes are gone, you can either add more money or just throw the phone away." He held up his hand in conclusion. "No contracts. Simple as that."

Jane felt the weight of the phone in her hand. It wasn't sleek and shiny like her husbands. It was simple and rather bulky. But one thing kept flickering in her mind.

"So, there is no way to track it?" she asked.

The kid raised an eyebrow to her and then offered a conspiratorial grin. "Nope."

Jane continued staring at the phone, trancelike. She spoke as if speaking to herself. "And I can just throw it away at any time and no one will know who it belonged to?"

"Yep."

Jane took a deep breath. It was wrong. Being here, at this kiosk, was wrong. Devon would not be pleased.

But Devon didn't have to know.

She bit her lip. "So, I give you cash and you activate the phone. And that's it?"

It felt like a scene that should be played out in a back alley somewhere and not in the middle of a bustling shopping mall.

"Well…" the young man started, and Jane looked up sharply.

He held up his hands. "You'd just have to register it if you want to add money. Or upgrade it, or anything. There's a website…"

For the first time in weeks, the fog in Jane's mind showed signs of clearing. She knew what she wanted to do. She stood up, holding out the phone and reached inside her purse. "How many minutes will $100 get me?"

Ten minutes later, Jane took the newly activated phone, shoved it into the bottom of her purse, and hurried away from the kiosk. As promised, she had not signed a thing and once the money had exchanged hands, the phone had been activated and handed over without further ado. Jane felt like she had just taken part in an illicit drug transaction rather than the purchase of a cell phone.

She had done it. She had decided and followed through.

Self-doubt crept in immediately.

If Devon ever found out, he would be enraged. The thought sent a little shiver down her spine.

It wasn't like she was going to use it, anyway. She would just carry it around for a little while and then throw it away.

No harm done.

Jane walked calmly back through the mall and into the parking lot. The bright sun shone down, and Jane squinted. The phone felt like a forbidden weight inside her purse. She tossed the bag of towels into the trunk of the car and then slid into the driver's seat.

The soft leather immediately comforted her. She reached down into her purse and pulled out the silver phone. It was heavier than the newest models and didn't have any bells or whistles. It wasn't even a touch phone. Just a regular phone with little more than a TALK and END button. Jane's heart raced as she contemplated the phone in her hand, and she mentally scolded her inner anxieties.

So what? She had bought a phone. It wasn't like she was going to call someone with it.

She didn't even have the phone number with her.

But she'd stared at it so many times, she knew it was ingrained in her memory.

She flipped up the top of the phone.

The push button numbers beckoned her brazenly. She typed in the area code. Each button made a little beep as she punched it in. She kept going, typing in the numbers she had lost so much sleep over. When all the digits were entered, she stared at the number and a wave of anger washed over her. How dare the person behind these numbers disrupt her life like that? In all these weeks, she had never once thought to be angry.

But suddenly, she was.

What was so special about this person that Devon would leave his own party to talk with? Jane wanted to know.

She truly did.

With trembling fingers, Jane hit TALK.

The phone rang.

Once.

Twice.

"Stephanie Logan."

Jane sucked in a deep breath. She had a name.

Her heart pounded in her chest and the realization of what she had just done sank in fully.

She took the phone away from her ear and stared at it in horror.

"Wait." She heard the voice from far away as she dropped the phone in her lap. "Don't hang up."

Jane put the phone back to her ear, but didn't speak.

"Are you there?" The woman's voice sounded calmer, although still urgent.

Jane took a deep audible breath to indicate that she was. She wasn't prepared to use her voice yet.

"Is this the same person that called me before? Do you know Devon?"

At the sound of Devon's name, Jane snapped the phone shut.

Chapter Seven

"Damn It," Stephanie said as she heard the click of the phone. This time she was certain the line was dead.

Shaking her head, she turned back to the stack of legal papers on her desk. Picking up her red pen, she started reviewing the contract before her. Within minutes, the words started to blur together, and Stephanie shut her eyes and took a deep breath. Her mind wandered back to the phone call. She had not recognized the phone number, but something in her gut told her it was the same person who had called before from Devon's number.

"Stop it," she scolded herself, turning the page in the contract and placing the tip of her pen over the first line. She was just being paranoid. There was absolutely no reason to think the two calls were related. That was probably just a wrong number, and she had completely overreacted. Except she had heard breathing on the other end of the line. Not creepy, I'm going to kill you breathing; but shallow breaths indicating someone was holding the phone to their ear, listening. Someone who was nervous or anxious.

"Ridiculous," she said, returning her concentration to her work. The breaths continued to nag at her brain. Why didn't they just say something? It seemed as if whoever was calling was intentionally trying to hear Stephanie talk. What did they want from her? To scare her? They'd have to do better than some light, timid breathing. Was Devon messing with her? She doubted that. Devon took himself way too seriously to play those kinds of games.

Stephanie tossed her pen across the desk in frustration. She was never going to get this contract reviewed with these random thoughts running through her brain.

"Everything okay in here?" her assistant popped her head into the door.

Stephanie snatched up the pen and nodded. "I'm fine."

Her assistant nodded and shuffled back out to her desk. Stephanie tapped the pen against her desk several times, but she knew her concentration was shot for good.

"Damn it," she said again and picked up her cell phone. There was really only one way to solve this mystery.

She hit redial on her phone.

It rang. Once. Twice. Three times.

No one answered. Stephanie sighed and took the phone from her ear. It was probably just a wrong number. She had an overactive imagination. People dialed wrong numbers all the time. And bots spam called cell phones randomly. Stephanie couldn't tell whether she was disappointed or relieved.

She reached down to press the red terminate button when she heard the line connect.

She raised the phone to her ear.

"Don't ever call this number. You can't call me." The voice was shrill, almost panicked.

"Whoa," Stephanie appealed, sitting up in her chair. She was alarmed by the panic in the woman's voice.

"Hold on a minute. You called me."

Stephanie waited, her own heart pounding. Gone was the timid breathing from before, replaced with rapid, erratic breaths. At least she hadn't hung up. Stephanie turned her chair around, so she faced the window in the back of her office.

"Who is this?" she tried, working to keep her voice from sounding threatening.

"If he hears the phone, he won't be pleased."

Stephane could hear the fear in her voice. Almost like a little girl, but Stephanie had a feeling this was an adult. "Okay, I hear you," she said. "I won't call you again. But can you tell me why you are trying to reach me?"

"Who are you?" The voice dropped to little more than a whisper.

Stephanie thought about her options for a moment. She could pretend it was a misunderstanding and just hang up and be done with it. But something in the woman's haunted voice made her feel like the woman deserved more. Taking a deep breath, she said simply, "My name is Stephanie Logan."

"How do you know my husband?"

Stephanie's heart skipped a beat. Deep down, she had known. But to hear it out loud felt like a hammer to her brain. This woman was married to Devon. Her Devon.

Suddenly, Stephanie felt like an imposter. It was fine to live in denial when there were no faces or voices attached. It was easy to pretend the other side of Devon's life didn't exist, or, at the very least, didn't concern her.

But here it was. And it did concern her.

And if the woman was as fragile as Devon made her

113

out to be, Stephanie was concerned she might break if she learned the truth.

Keeping her voice neutral, she said, "I'm his–" She couldn't help the pause. "His friend."

"You're sleeping with him."

There was no hesitation on the other end. It wasn't exactly an accusation, more of a statement of fact. Stephanie was a little surprised by the lack of hysterics. From Devon's indications, his wife was off balance and capable of cracking at any moment. Stephanie wasn't sure what to say. It made her uncomfortable as well.

"It's okay. You don't have to answer. I already know."

The woman's voice sounded much stronger than before and was far from fragile. An immense wave of guilt rushed over her. Stephanie, never at a loss for words, jogged her mind for something to say, maybe some sort of explanation. "I…uh…"

"Don't." The woman cut her off. "I'm sorry. I have to go. Don't call me again."

"Wait," Stephanie shouted into the phone, but the line was dead.

Staring at the blank screen for a long moment, Stephanie took deep breaths, trying to calm her racing heart. She felt as if she'd run a marathon. The muscles in her neck and jaw clenched like a vise. It was the nightmare she lived with every day come true. It was one thing to have an affair secretly and pretend everything was normal. It was something else completely to be called out on it by the very person who was being disrespected the most. Stephanie always considered herself a good person at heart–she was honest and loyal and yet, here she was, caught right in the middle of this enormous lie. What a hypocrite. She dropped her head, letting it fall into the palms of her hands. How had she let things get this far? She didn't want to hurt anyone–yet that was exactly what her actions had done. And if Devon found out….

Stephanie didn't even want to think of it.

Beside her, her phone vibrated. Stephanie raised her head and grabbed for the phone. The woman had called back. Stephanie wanted to make things right. Maybe not right, but better. She wanted to fix the mess she had created.

Breathlessly, she pushed the talk button without even looking at her screen. "I'm glad you called back. Can we talk about this?"

"Talk about what?"

Stephanie's heart stopped beating inside her chest. The voice on the other end was not the woman from before. It was Devon.

Her world stopped revolving as she stared at the screen, frozen. Did he know? Already? She shook her head. He couldn't know.

"Stephanie?" Devon's voice went from confused to annoyed. "What is going on?"

Stephanie pressed her lips together, struggling to regain her composure. If she spoke now, Devon would sense something was wrong. When he got a suspicion in his mind, he was like a dog with a bone. He never let it go. Stephanie was always very careful to keep any information, no matter how innocent, away from him that might make him jealous. It was sad, really, that a man cheating on his wife should be so suspicious of his mistress.

That thought spurred her out of her indecision. Let

him be annoyed. She was pretty annoyed herself. Taking that anger and channeling it into her voice, she said now, "Nothing is going on. I thought you were a client."

"Must be some client," he noted, sounding skeptical.

"It's fine," she reiterated, feeling irritated. "What did you need?"

She knew she was being rude, but it was the only thing saving her from freaking out completely and giving herself away.

"I thought it might be nice to hear your voice." His voice turned petulant–he clearly didn't appreciate her abrupt tone. To her, he sounded like a spoiled child. She knew he was trying to appeal to her sympathies–he did love to play the victim. Normally, she would capitulate just to keep the peace, but right now she wasn't interested in keeping the peace. She needed to get off the phone. If she stayed in this conversation for one more second, she was going to explode.

"I really need to go. I've got a meeting in about five minutes."

She hung up the phone, knowing there would be consequences for her actions. Devon didn't like being ignored. He'd wait until 10:30 or 10:45 to call her tonight, knowing she would be up waiting for him. And then he would be curt or rude and leave her feeling like she had misbehaved.

Stephanie felt anger start to well up inside her. She hated the fact that she allowed Devon to hold so much control over her. Sure, when they were together it was easy to get lost in the moment, but, at times, like this, when she took a step back and looked at the situation from afar, she realized how unfair the relationship was. Devon liked to pretend to be the victim, but she knew he was really the puppet master.

And she was the puppet. Or one of them, at least.

Stephanie began stacking the papers on her desk. Her chest felt heavy from the anxiety nestled there. But underneath the anxiety, a slow simmer burned.

She was tired of being a puppet.

Her paper stacking became more aggressive. She slammed the papers into a file folder and, opening a drawer, she began tossing folders inside. They weren't in the correct order and, no doubt, she would have an impossible time figuring out which papers went where, but right this second, she didn't give a damn. She wanted everything off her desk. She wanted things clean and simple. So what if she used her desk as a metaphor for her life? She needed to be in control of something. And she certainly wasn't in control of Devon.

Damn him, anyway, for putting her in this position.

"Doing a little housecleaning?"

Brad leaned against the doorframe to her office and gave her a smile. Stephanie jumped at the sound of his voice and then looked down at the files in her hand. Somehow, despite the chaos in her brain, it appeared to others as if she were going about her normal day. A little of the control crept back into her soul. Magically, some of the anxiety in her chest dissipated, and she managed a smile. "Something like that."

Nodding sympathetically, Brad commiserated, "I understand. One cannot function properly with too much clutter in their lives."

Stephanie could not hold back an ironic chuckle. If he only knew. "Words to live by," she muttered under her breath.

"Well," Brad straightened up and slid his hands into

the front of his jean's pockets. "When you're done cleaning, how about grabbing some dinner?"

Stephanie stopped mid file. Her instinct began searching for an excuse to decline. Dinner with a male, any male, even a colleague, no, especially a colleague, would not go over well with Devon. It would be easier for her to just make her excuses and go home to...

To what?

Wait for Devon to call?

Listen to him pout and whine about her abrupt behavior as if she were a child?

Is that what her life had become?

Her eyes held Brad's gaze. His eyes, like Devon's, were a rich chocolate brown, but, unlike Devon, Brad's eyes were warm and friendly, and open. He didn't have anything to hide.

As he watched her, Stephanie felt something flutter inside her chest. Something that hinted at – attraction.

Why shouldn't she have dinner with him? She was, after all, a single woman. And he was a single man. A very attractive single man, now that she thought about it. It's what single people did. Had dinner.

As the seconds of silence grew long, Brad straightened and said, "I understand if you already have plans. It's last minute..."

"No," Stephanie interrupted, a little too loud. Brad raised an eyebrow, and Stephanie felt herself blush. Lowering her voice, she added, "I mean, I was just thinking that it would be nice to go home and change first." She absently flicked a hand at her tailored jacket. "I've been in this suit all day."

"Great." Brad's eyes lit up, and he smiled widely. "I can pick you up, if you want."

Okay. Too much.

"Actually, it would be better if I just met you somewhere." She smiled apologetically, working furiously to come up with some plausible reason for needing her own car.

Turned out, she didn't need an excuse.

"Sure," Brad replied amicably. "Why don't we meet at Taverna? I know how much you love their risotto."

Taverna was a quaint Italian restaurant just blocks from the office, right in the heart of downtown. The attorneys in her office often took clients there for lunch. It was a great choice. A place that was charming and delicious and not in the least bit intimidating to Stephanie. He didn't know it, but Brad's suggestion had scored major points.

"Okay." Stephanie offered a smile. "I'll see you there–around 6:00. Is that okay?"

"Perfect." Brad gave her a smart salute and ambled back into the hallway.

Stephanie stalled for time at her desk for the next half hour. She certainly wasn't getting any work done, but she would be damned if she rushed out of the office like a giddy schoolgirl. She was a grown woman and this was just dinner. People did it all the time. No big deal.

"Oh, what the hell," she said out loud, reaching for her purse. If she left now, she had time to stop by the salon and have her hair blown out.

At six o'clock precisely, Stephanie stood in front of Taverna, that restaurant she wasn't in the least bit intimidated by, trying to calm her racing heart. She reached down and absently smoothed her draped silk top down over her dark skinny jeans. Her hair stylist, who had dropped everything once Stephanie explained that she had a date. Perfectly styled, her blonde hair was silky straight, but not overly so. The makeup artist, who happened to have a cancellation at that time, offered to touch up her makeup, giving it a "natural" look that was impossible for one to accomplish on her own. Now, two hours later, Stephanie did, literally, look like she had just stepped out of a salon.

"It's too much," Stephanie whispered to herself. She was going to scare this guy away–or give him the wrong impression, at the very least. Why didn't she just leave on her suit from work? Why did she have to turn it into something so dramatic?

"I'm so stupid," she muttered under her breath, on the verge of turning around and running back to her car. What was she doing here? She was going to make a complete fool out of herself. She should just leave and make up some excuse tomorrow.

"Hey." Brad came up beside her, placing a hand on her shoulder. He leaned in and gave her a friendly kiss on the cheek. "I'm glad you just got here. I was afraid I was going to be late."

He gave her a warm smile. Stephanie stared back, taken by surprise. She was mortified she had been discovered hovering in the doorway of the bar, considering the possibility of standing up this perfectly nice guy who only wanted to buy her dinner.

"Oh! Uh," she stammered and then said without thinking, "Hey, yourself."

Oh, God, it was her private greeting to Devon.

"I mean, 'hi yourself'," she corrected, trying to cover her flustered breathing. She shook her head and closed her eyes. How could it be getting worse? She felt about twelve years old. Taking a deep breath, she said firmly, "I mean, just 'hi'."

Stephanie was mortified at her own behavior. What was she doing? Rambling like a schoolgirl? Stephanie willed herself to get a grip. She was always calm and collected. She truly, truly did not want to embarrass herself in front of this great guy.

Luckily for her, Brad didn't seem to notice. "Let's get inside. I'm starving." As he reached for the door to the bar, he added, "You smell great by the way."

Her chest relaxed from the easy nature of Brad's personality. She could do this.

Once inside, she allowed the familiarity of the restaurant to comfort her.

"What do you get here?" Brad asked, studying the menu.

"The capellini pomodoro is really good," she said reflexively.

"Are you much of a risk taker?"

Stephanie looked up, concerned. "Why?"

Brad shook his menu. "Do you get the same thing every time?"

"Oh." Stephanie chuckled and placed her menu back on the table. "Yeah, pretty much."

Brad laughed. "Me, too."

The waiter arrived with a bottle of red wine that Brad had ordered, and Stephanie took a sip. The spicy flavor warmed her insides, and she let her guard down a tad.

Brad, on the other hand, was a natural at being relaxed. He sat back in his chair and took in the room and environment around them. The restaurant was bustling with activity, and he raised his voice so that he could be heard. "So, tell me something about yourself that I don't already know."

Stephanie blushed and lowered her eyes. If he only knew….her entire existence was a secret. She kept her professional and private life separate. Until now.

"I'm a runner," she started.

Brad raised his hands in mock exasperation. "Come on. I know that. I'm still sore from that 5K you made everybody run."

Stephanie laughed. Last year, she had gotten the company to sponsor a local 5K and had forced everyone on staff to take part. Most of the crew barely made it across the finish line and one particular colleague had stopped halfway through for a cigarette break.

"Okay. Okay." Stephanie gestured with her hands. "Calm down. Let me think…"

She tapped her fingers against the table. Luckily for her, she had more secrets than just Devon. And Brad was so open and friendly, she didn't mind sharing a few with him.

"Ah," she raised a finger. "How about this? I love….," she paused for dramatic effect. "NASCAR."

Brad blinked his eyes. "NASCAR? Really?"

Stephanie nodded. "Even won my Fantasy NASCAR league last year."

"Fantasy NASCAR? That is hardcore," Brad agreed. "Doesn't that take up quite a bit of time?"

"It does," she admitted. "But it gives me something to do until Fantasy Football starts up again."

"Whoa." Brad held a hand to his chest. "You play Fantasy Football?"

Stephanie couldn't help but laugh. Brad looked pleasantly surprised. She replied with false modesty, "Superbowl Champ three years in a row."

"Hmph," Brad said, raising an eyebrow. "Well, it's official now."

"What is?" she asked.

"You really are the perfect woman."

Stephanie laughed again. "Hardly. But I do like my sports. And I'm pretty competitive" Then, taking a sip of her wine, she asked. "How about you?"

"Well, I have never been to a NASCAR race," Brad admitted, "But I did get a speeding ticket last month; so, I've got that going for me."

Dinner came, and the two settled into relaxing banter as they finished off the wonderful meal. At one point, Stephanie looked around at the other diners enjoying their own private conversations and thought to herself how nice it was to be out at a restaurant having dinner with someone. She hadn't realized how much she missed keeping herself so private these last few years, eating alone and staying home to wait for Devon.

"Everything okay with your meal?" Brad asked.

She glanced down at her empty plate. "It appears so," she said, grinning.

Brad refilled her wine glass from a second bottle. Maybe it was the wine, maybe it was the company, but Stephanie couldn't remember the last time she felt so at ease. he wasn't ready for the night to end.

"We should come here more often," she blurted out. She was not the sort of person to be this forward, but this entire evening was everything she needed and more.

"Are you asking me out on a second date?" he asked. "Shouldn't we wait to see this night ends?" He grinned.

"You're right," she blushed. "Were you always this easygoing?"

Brad laughed. "I suppose so."

"What were you like as a kid?"

"Pretty much just like I am now."

"And how is that?" Stephanie asked.

He shrugged. "Responsible, driven, devastatingly handsome, irresistibly charming…."

Stephanie laughed. "Don't forget modest…"

Brad grinned and then said seriously, "You know, my dad worked his entire life as a contractor. He would budget our money every year and we would live and die by that budget. That taught me to be financially responsible, but I never wanted to be a slave to a budget. I vowed when I was twelve to be a millionaire by the time I was thirty."

"And…" Stephanie knew it was rude to ask, but she couldn't help herself.

"I turn thirty next month."

The way he spoke and the gleam in his eye left Stephanie no doubt that he had fulfilled his vow, or was close to it.

"What about you?"

"I turned thirty-six months ago. I am not a millionaire." She grinned. "But, you know what? I own my house. I have a nice little stock portfolio. I'm saving for my retirement. And I can buy any damn pair of shoes I want."

They laughed and toasted to new shoes.

"So, why is someone so perfect still single?"

Stephanie paused, her glass midway to her lips. The blunt nature of the question threw her for a loop. She was not prepared to lie to him on their first date, but there was no way she could tell him the truth. She struggled with how to answer. Say something funny? Something flippant? Something coy? Stephanie didn't know how to be any of those things.

Looking into his eyes, Stephanie realized Brad didn't care what she said or how she said it. He was interested in her and wanted to know more about her. She could probably tell him anything. Stephanie stopped herself. Anything – but that. With a bittersweet smile, she said, "I got divorced 5 years ago. It has taken me a while to get over it, I guess."

Brad watched her for a moment and then nodded his head thoughtfully. "That's good."

Stephanie stared back at him, perplexed by his nonchalant response. "Good?"

"Not good that you got divorced," Brad clarified. "Good that it took you a while to get over it."

She raised an eyebrow in question, and he explained more. "It means you took it seriously. That's the problem these days. It's too easy to walk away from things. If it doesn't hurt to let go, it wasn't worth having in the first place."

Stephanie nodded. "My husband left me for another woman. I was raised Catholic, and I don't, didn't," she corrected, "believe in divorce. But, in the end, what choice did I have? I didn't want to be divorced, but I also didn't want to be married to someone who didn't want to be married to me."

"Do you still believe?" Brad asked.

"In marriage?"

He nodded.

She nodded instantly. "Absolutely. Despite everything, I liked being married."

The deep subject matter felt heavy, weighing down the table. Brad paused in reflection for a minute and then smiled, "Yeah, me, too."

"You, too, what?" Stephanie asked.

"Like being married."

Stephanie almost choked on her water. "I didn't know you were married."

Brad blushed. "Oh, no, I'm not–I mean I never have been married. I just like the idea of being married." His eyes seemed to grasp onto her soul and pull her in. "I mean when you meet the right person–the one who completes you–what could be more beautiful than to experience everything in life together? Sounds like the perfect adventure to me."

Stephanie allowed herself to imagine it. She thought the person standing next to her would be Devon, but right now, all she could see was Brad. She smiled. "You're right. It does."

As the waiter cleared their plates and Brad poured the last of the wine, he asked, "Do you want dessert?"

Her initial response was to just say no, but then she had an idea. "Do you want to walk over to Maggie's down the street? They have the best homemade ice cream…"

Brad nodded immediately.

After quickly paying the bill, the couple stepped out onto the city sidewalk. Even though it was a weeknight, the city was bustling with people. The sky was clear and bright, and Stephanie felt alive with the energy around.

"Hey look," Brad pointed to where a tall thin man in an old-fashioned tux, complete with top hat and cane, stood on the corner of the sidewalk. "What do you think that's all about?"

Stephanie shook her head. She had no idea. She was never out and about downtown after dark. The hardcore bustle of Miami nightlife was not her scene.

Taking her hand, Brad led her in that direction. "Let's ask."

"I'm getting ready to lead the Walking Ghost Tour," the man said with a smile when approached. "We leave in about ten minutes."

"Are there many ghosts in this part of the city?" Stephanie asked.

The man nodded, his face lighting up. "Oh, yes. You'd be surprised at the stories these old buildings hold."

Brad looked at Stephanie. "Do you want to do it?"

A walking ghost tour had never even entered her radar as something to do on a date, but it sounded fun. And Brad would be the perfect companion. She shrugged her shoulders, but she knew her eyes were gleaming.

Brad turned to the man. "Do we have time to get ice cream?"

The man smiled. "I'm certain you do."

When they returned with dripping ice cream cones, a nice little group had gathered around the man with the top hat. Exchanging glances, they took their place in line, and the man gave them a wide smile. "I think we are all here. Shall we begin?"

As the small group crossed the street and took a turn down one of the alleyways, Brad reached down and took Stephanie's hand. His hand felt strong and warm in hers, and she was thankful he couldn't feel the sudden pounding of her heart. It was such a simple gesture, but it sent waves of electricity coursing through her soul. No one had taken her hand in such a manner, especially in a public setting, in a very, very long time.

"This is Castor manor," the leader stopped in front of an old stone brownstone, and the group gathered around him. Stephanie racked her brain trying to place the old shotgun-style building. She walked these streets almost every day, but honestly couldn't remember ever taking notice of this particular building.

"James Castor was the master of the manor. He was a wealthy man, a politician, and he had a wife and three children. He also had a mistress named Madeline. He kept Madeline hidden in the basement." The man tapped his cane in the direction of the low, long window at the bottom of the building. "This was the only view of the outside that Madeline ever had. Granted her basement apartment was nicely furnished, and Madeline had the finest clothing for when James would visit her, he expected the same comforts of his own home, but she was only allowed outside of the apartment when the missus and children were safely away."

Stephanie felt a shiver run down her spine. Mistaking it for a chill, Brad put his arm around her shoulders and rubbed her arm. Stephanie didn't correct him. His caress felt too nice.

"History has it that one night, upstairs in the main house, a torch tipped over setting the heavy curtains on fire. James hustled his family into the carriage outside and fled the burning building, safe and sound. But he completely forgot his mistress locked in the basement downstairs. If he had turned back, he might have noticed Madeline pounding on the basement window, the last vision before she died seeing the man she loved riding away.

Even though the apartment has since been completely gutted and rebuilt, the current owners say they can still hear the wails coming from the basement on a cold, winter night."

Stephanie shuddered and turned away. Somehow, the story struck a chord with her. Metaphorically, wasn't she really Madeline? She was locked inside a basement of her own making, and Devon was the master. If the house burned down, would Devon even think twice about leaving her there?

"Are you okay?" Brad asked.

She wasn't. She suddenly felt slightly nauseous. She started to play it off, but the shaking in her voice gave her away. "I don't know if I'm cut out for this ghost story business."

"It's most likely all made up, you know," he offered with a smile. The group had moved on, but Stephanie made no attempt to join them.

Inexplicably, she felt tears sting her eyes. "It's just so sad."

"Hey," Brad's tone softened. "You're really not okay. What's wrong?"

"She loved him, and he left her," she exclaimed, dangerously close to erupting into full sobs. "He just left her."

Brad enveloped her in his arms. Smoothing down her hair, he crooned, "It's okay. It was just a story. It's okay."

After a moment, Stephanie pulled herself together enough to step out of Brad's embrace. She wiped her eye and said, "I'm sorry…I guess that story just struck a nerve…"

He knew she was divorced, and she just prayed that he assumed that was what she was referring to.

Placing his hands on her shoulder, he stared into her eyes. "For the record, if I were James and I was lucky enough to have you love me, I would never leave you."

His words were so direct and so honest that Stephanie felt the tears well up again. She smiled at him through blurry eyes. "You know what? I believe that is true."

Brad smiled at her. "Good." He let his hand linger on her cheek before saying. "Looks like the group left us." Sure enough, the street around them was empty. He smiled. "What should we do now?"

Stephanie made the mistake of looking at her watch. It was eleven o'clock. Reality came rushing back. She had missed her 10:00 call. She felt like a disobedient teenager.

In a rush, the peaceful feeling slid away, and her usual cloak of anxiety settled back in. Giving Brad a sympathetic look, she said, "It's late. I should really get home."

"Are you sure?" Brad looked disappointed.

She was disappointed as well, but growing more alarmed over her situation by the second. She had damage control to do. "I'm sure," she declared.

Brad gave her a disarming smile. "Can we at least plan on doing it again?"

She hoped so. Oh, God, she hoped so.

Standing on her tiptoe, she kissed Brad. It was meant to be more of a friendly gesture. An *I had a nice time* kind of thing. But when her lips touched his, an electricity she wasn't expecting soared through her veins. She gasped and when she tried to pull away, Brad put his hand on her neck and held her close. She didn't protest. She was entranced by the way he moved his lips coaxingly across hers. There was no demand; no urgency like she was used to. Brad's kiss was slow and lingering, as if he had all the time in the world. He didn't have a concern in the world that they were standing on a street corner in the middle of the city. He didn't care who might walk by or who might take notice. He was a man kissing a woman, and he didn't care who knew it.

It was refreshing and terrifying at the same time. She hadn't felt so free and so relaxed in literally years; but at the same time she hated to think of what that freedom might cost her. Devon was the ultimate selfish lover. He would not commit to her, but he would never allow her to commit to someone else. In the past, it had not been worth the risk, but, somehow, in this moment, with Brad, she felt differently. Maybe, just maybe, Brad was worth the risk.

Gently, she broke off the kiss. Brad groaned good-naturedly. "What? You're not a fan of kissing in the middle of the street?"

She blushed, but smiled and admitted shyly, "Actually, I quite liked it."

"I did, too." His face softened, and he smiled at her in a new, sexy way that sent shivers up her spine. "I can continue if you want."

She wanted to, but she also knew if she started something with Brad right now, she wouldn't want it to end with just a kiss. She was already walking too fine of a line. To be fair, she needed to sort out her situation before she started anything serious with Brad. He deserved her full attention. She wouldn't do to him what was being done to her by Devon.

With a sigh of regret, she stepped out of Brad's embrace. "I really need to get home."

Never one to push, Brad nodded his head and conceded gracefully. "Can I at least see you home?"

But Stephanie was shaking her head before he even

got the words out. She wasn't ready to take that kind of step. Besides, she wasn't sure what she might have waiting for her at home.

Anticipating her answer, Brad said, "Well, then, I'll walk you to your car and let you be on your way."

As they walked the short blocks to her car, Brad held her hand comfortably. To him, it was probably an insignificant gesture, but Stephanie found herself treasuring the simple closeness. It felt so good to be open and carefree. She felt in her heart something had happened tonight that would change her forever. She wanted this feeling.

She gave Brad a goodnight kiss, praying it was only the first of many, and then slid into her car. Brad stood on the sidewalk and waved as she pulled away from the curb.

Suddenly, the phone on the seat next to her vibrated.

Stephanie jumped as if she had been physically assaulted.

Her heart pounded wildly in her chest. She had left her phone in the car for this very reason. She didn't want to be connected to Devon during her date with Brad. But now, reality set in. It was now 11:30.

With a sinking feeling in the pit of her stomach, Stephanie glanced at the phone lying on the seat next to her. The screen was lit with the letters DCELL. It was her code name for Devon. Underneath it were the words *43 missed calls*.

It was worse than she thought.

For the rest of the drive home, Stephanie felt a sense of panic rising in her throat. What if Devon were at her house waiting for her? What would she do? She wouldn't stop, she decided. It would be too dangerous. She'd run straight to the police.

Stephanie slammed on the brakes as the light in front of her changed to red. This was crazy. Was that how one was supposed to feel about a person she supposedly loved? Afraid? Ready to go to the police?

Of course, it wasn't. She had known that for a long time. Tonight, for the first time though, she had a taste of what normal could be like. It made the inappropriateness of her current situation more glaring.

Nearly sick to her stomach with anxiety, Stephanie pulled the car down the dark alley behind her condo. She crept the car along the road at a snail's pace, her heart thumping so loudly she felt it would burst from her chest. Time moved in slow motion as she pulled past her neighbor's fence to her own drive.

It was empty.

Her relief was so immense that she literally sagged over the steering wheel of the car. She took a couple of deep breaths and quickly pulled her car into the garage as if she were afraid Devon would emerge from the bushes at any time.

Safely inside, Stephanie showered, changed into her pajamas, and crawled into bed. Instead of happily reliving her kiss with Brad, she found herself staring at the screen of her phone. 43 missed calls. Her inbox mail envelope indicated she had new messages. She could only guess what they contained.

...Its after 10:00, I was just calling to say good-night.

...Its 10:15, I'm wondering where you are

...Its 10:17, I'm getting worried, hope everything is okay

...Its 10:19, where are you?

And so on.

As she scrolled through the messages, the phone vibrated in her hands, lighting up and causing her to jump out of her skin. She looked at the clock. 11:50. If she answered, what would she say? What excuse would she make? Regardless of what she came up with, Devon would be suspicious, and the conversation would not be pleasant.

A surge of anger rose in her throat. How dare Devon ruin her evening? She immediately revised that thought. Devon was only doing what she had allowed for far too long. It was her choice. And, starting right this second, she lived her own life. She no longer wanted Devon to control it. She looked down at the phone once more. 44 missed calls.

It was time to take control of her life. She pressed the power button on the phone, turning the screen black.

Starting right now.

Chapter Eight

Jane blinked groggily as the bedroom was flooded with light. Raising a hand to shield her sensitive eyes from the brightness, she sat up in bed glancing at the clock on the nightstand. It was midnight. Her head still thick with sleep, she turned her head to the door, curious what had caused the sudden intrusion on her slumber.

Her husband stood in the doorway.

She could tell from there that his eyes were black.

A trickle of apprehension ran down her spine. She sat up and pulled the covers to her chest. "Devon? Is something wrong?"

She couldn't imagine what could have upset him at this hour. Things had been fine all evening. Dinner had gone without comment. They had watched a new episode of his favorite cooking show. Afterward, they had both gone to bed–her with a book and him with the newspaper. Yes, Devon had left the room sometime after ten o'clock, but there had been no animosity in his departure and, soon afterward, Jane had gone to sleep.

Clearly, something had changed.

Devon stalked across the room, a little unsteady on his feet, and demanded, "Pull down the covers." When she hesitated, he sneered, "Are you afraid of me?"

She lowered the covers immediately, shaking her head; but it was too late.

He stalked toward the bed and yanked the covers

off, saying menacingly, "Maybe you should be." Jane recoiled at both the venom in his voice and the smell. He reeked of alcohol.

She wondered what had happened. Devon had had a glass of wine with dinner as usual, but his breath smelled like whiskey, something he rarely drank and certainly not alone in his office at this hour. Like most people, alcohol enhanced Devon's inherent personality traits. In this case—anger. She tried not to shrink away as Devon leaned across her caressing her shoulder roughly. Then he stopped and stared at her.

"Didn't you wear this nightgown last week?" He growled. He snapped the thin strap holding it on her shoulder, breaking it.

It was actually brand new, but she didn't say anything. Instead, she held the thin fabric against her skin and asked quietly, "Is everything all right?"

"No," he said, glaring at her. His voice sounded low and dangerous. Jane swallowed thickly. He moved his face right up against hers. She could feel the heat from his breath against her face. "Everything is not all right. I thought I asked you this morning to dust all the furniture."

"I did," she said, careful not to move her face from his. It would only increase his anger. No way he was this upset about dusting. The house, as usual, was spotless. She had, in fact, spent three hours wiping imaginary dust off of every piece.

Devon reached out like a snake and cupped her chin in his hands. Hard. "Don't lie to me."

With the strength of his grip on her face, she was unable to open her mouth to respond. Devon wasn't listening anyway. Thrusting her back against the headboard, he got out of bed and stalked over to the nightstand, picking up the lamp centered there. Holding it up to the light, he said with disdain, "Then what is this?"

It was a modern glass lamp that didn't have so much as a smudge on it. Jane leaned forward to inspect the piece. Honestly, she couldn't find one thing to say.

Her hesitation displeased Devon. He turned and shoved the lamp in her direction. "This lamp is filthy. Do you need a lesson in housekeeping?"

Jane shook her head, but before she could respond, he gripped the lamp so hard it shattered in his hand.

She scrambled out of bed and reached for his hand, which was bleeding in several places. "Let me get a washcloth."

He pushed her away. "You've done enough, don't you think?"

"Devon, I…" she started meekly.

He shook his head and headed toward the bathroom. "Clean this mess up."

Without hesitation, Jane scurried from the bed, still holding her torn nightgown in place. She gathered the shards of broken glass and put them into the small trash bin by their bed. When the sound of the water running in the bathroom reached her ears, she grabbed her robe to cover herself. She took the trash can downstairs and emptied the glass pieces into the bin outdoors. She didn't know what had caused his outburst, but she did know that Devon would not want to be reminded of it when he woke up in the morning. She only prayed the worst of it was over.

Wiping the bin dry, she returned upstairs, hoping to replace it before Devon was finished with his shower.

Instead, she found her husband lying in bed with his hands folded behind his head. Waiting for her.

Even though her heart pounded uncontrollably, Jane calmly set the trash can in its exact position next to the nightstand. Since there was no longer a lamp on the table, she asked quietly, "Would you like me to turn off the overhead light or did you want to read for a while?" She hoped that, by keeping a calm appearance, she could prevent any further incidents.

"I want you to get down on your knees and suck my dick."

She was wrong.

Okay, she told herself, gearing up mentally for whatever was in store for her. You can do this. He's your husband.

Without comment, she grasped the waistband of his pajama bottoms and pulled them down. His penis was full and erect and seemed to be staring at her in disdain as well.

She got to her knees on the bed and ran her tongue down the side of his shaft. She raised her eyes to his face as she did so because he liked to know she was paying attention to him at all times. He didn't appreciate what he called "going through the motions", even though that was exactly what she was doing. After making clear eye contact, she dropped her eyes and took all of him in her mouth. He groaned. That was a good sign. Most of the time, he tried his hardest to prolong the experience. He liked to see her work to keep him aroused even if he had to sacrifice some of his own pleasure. It was a twisted cycle.

Even though she knew better - he liked long slow strokes, she increased her rhythm following full mouth enclosure with quick hand strokes. It was a killer combination she knew he enjoyed.

Within moments, she could feel him writhing above her. He took his hands and placed them on her head, pushing her farther down on him. Luckily, Jane had plenty of experience–she relaxed her throat muscles and took as much as she could. It was amazing to think she had only been with one man her whole life. She had the skills of a professional. Devon had made sure of it. He might be seeing another woman, but she highly doubted anyone else could be trained to please Devon the way she was. She couldn't even comprehend what had comprised a normal relationship between a man and a woman. Devon was all she had ever known.

She increased the rhythm of her movements even faster, moving her hand down the length of his straining shaft. She could tell by his jerky movements he was close to climaxing. Sure enough, with a loud groan, Devon clamped his hand to the back of her head and held it in place as he relieved himself inside her mouth. He used a great deal of pressure to keep her head still although she had been trained over the years not to move. It would never have occurred to her to do anything differently. Sometimes Devon just liked to inflict a little extra pain.

Feeling the thick salty liquid on her tongue made her stomach clench, but Jane quickly swallowed and licked her lips clean. Even when he made the mess, Devon didn't like any reminders of it.

Once he was done, Devon immediately rose from the bed, knocking Jane to the side, and moved into the bathroom.

Relieved, Jane reached for her robe to cover herself. "What are you doing?"

Devon's voice coming from the bathroom entrance startled Jane, and she jumped. He had stopped and was staring at her.

"I was just getting my robe," Jane explained, flustered. Devon always showered after sex as if he couldn't stand having any reminder of her on him. She expected him to shower as always and then retire to his office. In fact, she had been counting on it. But, as she watched him, he returned to the bed and towered over her as she lay. When she looked up, she could see that his eyes were still black.

He shook his head at her, grinning maliciously. "You aren't going to need that just yet."

"But…" Hadn't she just pleased him? She couldn't help but glance at his flaccid penis. He didn't appear to be in shape for any further activities any time soon.

He followed her gaze and then laughed. "You did such a good job pleasing me. It wouldn't be fair if you didn't get the same satisfaction."

"Oh," Jane started. She didn't know what he was getting at. He rarely pleased her and even then only when she had been very, very good. Somehow, she doubted he was trying to make up with her. "I'm fine. Really."

Devon sat up in bed and ran his fingers along the ridge of her shoulder. She shivered. There was no pleasure involved with his touch.

He leaned back again and placed his hands behind his head. "Frankly, I'm too tired to participate. I'll just watch you pleasure yourself."

It wasn't a question. There was no desire in his voice. Devon knew Jane was most uncomfortable with visual displays. She could take the aggression, the roughness, even the physical pain. But to be exposed and

140

vulnerable in front of him was a torture for her she absolutely dreaded.

"And get that expression off your face," Devon snarled. "Try for god's sake to have some sex appeal. The 'deer in the headlights' act is getting old."

Jane straightened up, immediately placing a hooded expression on her face. His nasty tone touched a nerve. It must not have occurred to him that she looked scared because she was scared of him. What did he want from her? She had done everything he liked, just the way he liked–and it still wasn't enough. There was never enough punishment or humiliation to satisfy him.

And yet, despite everything, he left her and went to someone else. Someone who couldn't possibly satisfy him the way she did. Did he dare talk to his mistress that way? She let some of that anger slide up her spine. He wanted a show, did he? Well, good. She didn't want him touching her. In all the years she had known him, Jane had never once, not one time, intentionally talked back to Devon. She wasn't raised that way. And she understood the consequences.

Devon watched her contemplate her options. She knew he understood how uncomfortable she was. She also knew she had no choice. To disobey him would only result in further pain. A little humiliation, on the other hand, and hopefully she could put this night behind her.

Crawling up the bed on her hands and knees, Jane removed the silk belt from her robe and slid it around Devon's wrist, careful to avoid the cut from earlier that he had wrapped in gauze. His eyes widened at her bold move, but he didn't resist.

Leaning close to his face, she whispered, "This is for you."

When Devon didn't respond, she proceeded to tie his wrists to the bedpost, not tight enough to provide any restraint, but enough so that he couldn't easily grab her.

She slid back down and off the bed. She dropped her robe. She slowly allowed herself to sway to an internal music playing in her head. She ran her hands over her body, feeling the softness of her skin. It wasn't that she didn't know how to pleasure herself. She was perfectly in tune with her body. She ran her hands along her breasts. They were not huge, but natural and soft. She tweaked her nipple, feeling it grow taught. A heavy groan distracted her movements. She lifted her head and turned toward the bed.

Devon watched her with interest. He pulled at the ties confining him, and his eyes looked dark and dilated.

Seeing his blatant stare threw her off a little, and Jane fidgeted from one foot to the other. Maybe she wasn't as brave as she thought she was.

"Well?" The smirk was back, and she could see that he thought he had won.

"If you move, I'll stop," Jane said in a soft voice.

"Excuse me?" Devon sat up, straining at the ties. His gaze turned threatening.

Jane didn't back down. "I'm giving you what you asked for. Just sit back and enjoy it." She kept her voice soft, but her expression was firm. If he got up, she was going to run. She wasn't going to let him touch her – not tonight. Maybe not ever again.

After a moment, he lay back against the pillows and gestured a hand to her. "Go ahead."

Jane closed her eyes, blocking out Devon from her vision. He had set the tone, but it was up to her to perform.

She created a scene in her head. One she had imagined many, many times before. One where her lover, even if he didn't have a face, had gentle hands and a loving smile.

She didn't dare open her eyes for fear of what she would see. She had never let Devon see that deep inside of her. She rarely let herself go there. He only saw the puppet he trained. He only cared about his own pleasure. Instead, she let her imaginary lover take her to places only safe inside her head.

She didn't actually have an orgasm, turned out she didn't need to. Within moments, she heard a loud groan from the bed and when she finally opened her eyes, Devon had managed to come again, the sticky substance a small pool of white on his stomach.

Sliding on her silk robe, Jane calmly walked to the bed and pulled the silk tie from around his wrist. She cinched it around her waist. Then she went to the sink and wet a washcloth. She placed on her husband's chest without a word. And, leaving the robe firmly in place, she slid into bed, put her back to her husband, and went to sleep.

When Jane woke the next morning, Devon was gone.

Chapter Nine

6:45 AM

Stephanie sat on the bay window ledge of her living room, staring out at daylight crawling through the darkness.

She had been in this position for hours.

Her phone had stopped vibrating just before midnight, but she had not slept for fear that at any moment he would show up at her door. The closer it came to sunrise, the more likely he was to show up. In her mind, it was not a question of if, but when.

She took a sip of coffee, ice cold, but didn't taste anything. Her mind was swirling with the implications of her actions last night. She had gone over and over in her mind the conversation they might have. A conversation about truth and commitment and how she wanted those things. All her arguments seemed so logical – after all, was it so unusual for a woman to want to be in a relationship with a man who was actually available? She was perfectly within her rights, and Devon really didn't have a leg to stand on. But she knew it would never be that easy. It never mattered who was right or wrong-Devon always saw himself as the victim. She just wanted to keep him from being angry.

At 7:00, as the sun finally began its accent over the horizon, she saw headlights appear in her driveway.

Stephanie sighed and swung her legs off the ledge.

She wore faded blue jeans and an oversized T-shirt. She was going to lie to Devon, and she hoped that her lack of makeup and red swollen eyes would merely add to the conviction. She knew it was the cowardly way out, but she was exhausted mentally and physically.

She opened the door just as Devon was raising his hand to knock. He rushed in and put his hands on her shoulders. She winced at the pressure of his grip.

"I was worried about you last night. Did you get my messages?" On the surface, his expression was one of concern, but his eyes, dark and penetrating, held her gaze. He watched her carefully despite the soft caress on her cheek.

She had to hold her breath to keep from flinching at his touch. She felt a tension in the air that concerned her. Careful to keep her expression neutral, she offered the response she had been practicing all night. "I know. I took an Advil PM for a headache and fell asleep. I didn't realize my battery was low until I woke up this morning and saw that the phone was dead." She held it up, knowing the red low battery indicator would be on–she had let it drain all night. She put on what she hoped was a sheepish expression. "I feel so stupid. I hope you weren't too worried."

He watched her for a long time. She bit her bottom lip and strove for an innocent look. She didn't like Devon's expression, but prayed her fear didn't show on her face. Finally, Devon smiled, even though the smile didn't reach his eyes. "Well, I was worried. I didn't sleep very well wondering if you were okay."

He caressed her cheek again, but the pressure was a little too firm. "I hope you are feeling better now."

She shuddered at his touch and covered by raising a

hand to her forehead. "I am, thank you."

Stephanie heard a tremble in her own voice and it upset her. She didn't like feeling afraid, but more importantly, she didn't want Devon to think she was afraid.

Devon pulled her into his arms and whispered, "I know what will make us both feel better."

Stephanie felt herself stiffen in response. The last thing she wanted to do was make love. Not only was she exhausted from the long night, but being with Devon felt almost like a betrayal to the purity of her budding relationship with Brad, especially so soon after their date last night. A million excuses floated around in her head, but she knew Devon would not believe any of them. She had never, in all of their years together, turned him down.

"Don't even think about saying no," Devon whispered, as if he were reading her very thoughts. His grip on her arm was firm, and Stephanie felt if she resisted he would force himself on her.

Still, she scrambled for some reason to delay. Did he know when she last had her period? She knew he hated anything messy.

Devon must have sensed her hesitation because he gave her a pointed look and challenged with a sneer, "Are you coming?"

Stephanie felt her dread, like a lead weight on her chest. But she followed him to the bedroom. Inside, Devon shut the door and removed his tie. He stood before her, expectantly.

"I should change," she blurted out, desperately stalling for time.

As she made a reach for the bathroom, he shook his head and grabbed her arm, pulling her to the bed.

If he felt any of her reluctance, he ignored it. Instead, he unbuttoned her blue jeans and pulled them down over her hips. For the first time, Stephanie was disappointed she was not wearing panties. Devon didn't seem to notice either way. Leaving her jeans around her ankles, he pushed up her sweatshirt and fondled her breasts. There was nothing gentle or loving in his touch. After a moment, he moved over her belly and down to her exposed bottom. He spent a few moments caressing her with his fingers, accompanied by the occasional flick of his tongue. From her detached state, Stephanie could not muster a response. Normally, she would be concerned about Devon's needs and the way he wanted things done, but he didn't even seem to notice her indifference. After a few moments, he stood up, undid his fly, lowered his pants, and entered her, thrusting sharply inside her. He did not make eye contact. Stephanie closed her eyes to avoid seeing him thrusting on top of her. If he knew that she had made no movement whatsoever, he either wasn't going to acknowledge it, or simply did not care.

Stephanie remained in a state of disbelief. This? This was the man she loved? Pumping away on top of her without a glimmer of concern for her well-being. This was the man she had given up so much of her life for?

In that instant, the glass house she had so carefully constructed shattered around her.

She wasn't in love with Devon. At least not anymore. Last night, she had seen a brief glimpse of what true love could be like. Pure and innocent. The love she so desperately wanted was right at her fingertips.

And here she was, still at the mercy of a man who didn't belong to her. Who had never belonged to her…

Why did she stay?

She knew the answer. She stayed because she was afraid. Afraid of the control he exercised. If she didn't do something soon, she was going to lose any chance of happiness she might ever have.

Devon spent himself and rolled off her onto the bed beside her. With a grimace, she pulled down her sweatshirt. She hadn't had sex with her clothes on since college.

"Thanks for stopping by," she said sarcastically as he sat on the edge of the bed and reached for his shoes, one of the few things he had removed before he had taken advantage of her.

Luckily, her sarcasm came out a bare whisper as Devon turned back to give her a hard stare. "What did you say?"

Stephanie merely shook her head and stood up to put her jeans back on. Beside her, Devon ran a hand through his thick hair. A glimpse of white caught her attention. She buttoned her jeans and took a closer look. A white bandage covered the palm of his hand. She hadn't noticed it when he walked in, but now she could see the faint red stain where blood was congealed. This was no minor cut. She turned his hand, face up, and fingered the white gauze. For the first time, she looked up into his face. "What happened?"

Devon snatched his hand from hers. He looked almost as surprised as she was to see a bandage on his hand. He stooped down and retrieved his tie from the bedpost and quickly put it back on. When he faced her again, his smug expression was firmly in place. He waved his hand in a dismissive gesture and said, "When I couldn't reach you, I broke a lamp." He shook his head in mock regret, but his voice had a steely tone. "I have such a temper when I get upset. I just can't help it." He held her gaze captive with dark black eyes. "Things get broken."

Stephanie felt the hair on her neck rise. Who was this man? This man who used cruel words and sex to control her?

Before she could say anything further, Devon retied his tie and said, "I have an early meeting this morning."

Stephanie stared open-mouthed. Five minutes ago, he was practically forcing her to have sex.

Well, that was fine with her. She nodded her head and clenched her fists together in an effort to keep it together for just a moment longer.

Five minutes later, she was alone.

Stephanie sank down onto the sofa and let out a sob. She felt like she had narrowly escaped a horrifying nightmare.

A vision of the bandage came to mind. The cut underneath had been deep enough to seep through the thick gauze. Had he really broken a lamp? Or done something even more despicable?

How do you know my husband?

His wife's voice filled her brain, like a blurry form swirling through the depths of her mind.

You're sleeping with him.

I have such a temper when I get upset.

The voices danced and screamed inside her head. Stephanie dropped her head into her hands and sobbed. What if he had hurt his wife? What if her actions had caused pain for another woman? Stephanie picked up her phone from the coffee table. It was dead from last night. She jogged to the kitchen to find the charger. Even though Devon had not physically touched her, her body felt bruised and broken.

As the phone charged, Stephanie contemplated her options. She had to know if his wife; she knew her name was Jane, was all right.

Stephanie tossed the phone back and forth from one hand to the other, contemplating the right course of action.

She had an idea.

She scrolled through her recent call history until she found the one she was looking for. Punching in Options, she pressed the text button and typed: ARE YOU OKAY?

She hit send before she could have any second thoughts.

Chapter Ten

Jane was putting away laundry in the bedroom when her purse vibrated on the chair inside her closet. She set down the stack of shirts and reached for her purse. For an instant, she couldn't imagine what on earth was going on. There was no sound. If she hadn't been standing right next to it in the quiet closet, she would have never even noticed. But, without question, there was a soft buzzing coming from her purse. Like a razor, or a....

And then, suddenly, she knew.

Reaching into the bottom of her bag, she removed the cell phone.

The glowing screen indicated she had 1 message.

It took some finagling, but Jane finally managed to figure out the text screen.

ARE YOU OKAY?

She didn't have to look. She knew where it came from.

Her husband's lover.

Why was this stranger asking if she was okay?

And then the image of the broken vase. The blood on his hand flashed through her mind.

This woman knew about the cut.

Surely, she couldn't. Not this quickly. Maybe she was talking about something else. Jane typed furtively.

WHAT DO YOU MEAN?

A little longer time passed, but eventually, the phone

lit up.

I SAW THE CUT ON HIS HAND.

Jane felt as if she had been punched in the stomach. When Jane had woken up this morning, relieved to be alone, her husband had been at his lover's. Jane swallowed a lump in her throat. He had wasted no time in rushing to see his lover. This wasn't just some fleeting affair. This was a serious relationship.

She stared at the text again.

Jane hadn't looked at the cut since it happened, but it must have been deep enough to cause concern. Enough concern that this woman, her enemy, felt compelled to check on her.

Even though she should have been angry, Jane felt a hot tear trail down her cheek. Quite simply, no one had asked or cared about her well-being in a long, long time.

With shaking fingers, Jane typed in a response.

I'M OKAY.

As she hit the send button, she had another thought. What if Devon took out the same anger on someone else? Someone who didn't know how to handle him? Jane looked down at her phone. She had to know. She didn't want to be responsible for someone else getting hurt.

ARE YOU?

After a moment, the screen lit up again.

YES.

Good. Then it was settled. Jane knew she should just put the phone away and be done with this. It was dangerous territory, and it could only lead to disaster. But she had so many questions.

Of all the questions; however, only one really mattered.

HOW LONG HAVE YOU BEEN WITH MY

HUSBAND?

This time the silence was much longer. She wondered if the woman would deny it. Or ignore it?

Jane was about to give up when the phone lit up again.

FOR A LONG TIME.

This time, Jane didn't bother to respond.

She disconnected the phone and dropped it into her lap. The small phone suddenly felt as heavy as a weighted cannonball.

Jane sat silently in her closet for a long time as the impact of the conversation hit her. Her husband had a mistress. Someone who had been a part of his life for a long time. Jane didn't know what that meant–weeks, months, years, but it devastated her to the core.

Suddenly, everything she thought was stable in her life shook like an earthquake had hit. She went into her bedroom and removed her shirt. She ran her fingers over the blue marks on her arms and on her thighs. Images flashed through her mind–the biting comments, the roughness, the insults. She imagined last night's rampage and probably countless others had been fueled by another woman.

A feeling of something akin to jealousy swept through her. She bet he didn't speak to his mistress the way he spoke to her. No, he was probably charming and loving. No wonder she had been with him "a long time". He saved his best parts for someone else, leaving Jane with the fallout.

Feeling as if she had leaped off a tall building, Jane struggled to stand up. She held the phone in her hand as if it were a snake about to bite. Part of her wanted to just take it outside to the dumpster and dispose of it once and for all. Pretend none of this had ever happened.

But she knew that wasn't possible.

It had happened.

And as much as she didn't want to face it, she knew that it wasn't over.

A chain reaction had been ignited, and there was no one who could stop it now.

Looking around her closet, Jane searched for a place to put her phone. Leaving it in the bottom of her purse simply wouldn't do. Her closet was also tricky. Devon was prone to rummaging through her clothes while picking out outfits that were acceptable.

On the top shelf, the corner of a floral box caught her attention.

Jane drug the step stool and climbed to the top, stretching to grasp the box pushed back in the corner. Finally, she maneuvered the box down and held it in her lap. It was a medium-sized box covered in a pink floral pattern. That box contained mementos of her mother. It was one place she knew Devon would not search. He had never met her mother, but, somehow, had decided he didn't like her and wouldn't allow Jane to even speak of her around him. In fact, he had tried to make her get rid of the box several years ago, and it was one of the few battles she had fought and won. There had been a price, of course, she had been bruised for weeks, but it had been worth it in the end.

Feeling the lump in her throat grow, Jane removed the lid. On top were her mother's papers, a copy of her will, and several other items. Devon hid all of the originals in his office; but she had felt the need to keep a copy close to her. Removing those items, Jane stared lovingly at the trinkets inside.

There were three jewelry boxes containing a ruby ring, a pair of gold earrings and a classic pearl necklace. Jane opened the first velvet-lined box and slid the ring on her finger. It sparkled even in the dim light of her closet. Jane felt an immediate warmth surround her as if her mother had entered the room. Her mother's jewelry had been of the highest quality, but Devon would never let her wear them, and Jane wouldn't dream of selling them. Leaving the ring on, she reached for a stack of photographs she had salvaged from her mother's room. Her father had destroyed most of them after she died, and Devon took care of the rest, but she had held on to several she had found on her mother's nightstand. There was one of her and her mother on the beach, probably in South Carolina. Her mother had been young and very beautiful, with large, haunted eyes not unlike Jane's. Another picture was of the family, her father standing tall and straight without a hint of a smile, and her mother looking down at her as a small child with a loving protective gaze.

Tears slid down her face as she thumbed through the photographs. She had missed so much after her mother died. Her mother had been a beacon in the strict household where she grew up. Her favorite time as a child had been early in the morning, when she first awoke, her mother would come in and lay down next to her in her bed and wrap her arms around, holding her close. Her father didn't like to be disturbed in the morning, and Jane had learned at a very young age to keep any crying or discomfort to herself.

The last item in the box was a small wooden box with blue glass on top. It wasn't much to look at, but on her deathbed, her mother had pressed it into her hands and whispered with her soft, pain-filled voice, *"This is yours. Don't let anyone see it. Not your father or anyone else that might come into your life. This is my gift to you. When you need me, reach for this box and hold it close. I will come for you."*

"Oh, mother," Jane cried aloud, clutching the box to her bosom. "I need you."

As she lifted the box to her cheek, she heard a clatter inside the box. She turned it around and opened the lid. It was empty as it always had been.

Jane shook the box. Again, the clatter.

"What could that be?"

She turned it this way and that and then, seeing nothing unusual, peered inside once more. Using her index finger, she pressed on the bottom of the box. It immediately gave way to another compartment.

Jane sat back in astonishment. Inside that small box with the hidden compartment was a single key with a folded piece of paper. With trembling hands, Jane unfolded the paper. Inside, she discovered a street address and a set of numbers. Nothing more.

Jane turned the paper backwards and forwards, checked the entire box once more until she was satisfied there was nothing further to find.

She held the key in her hand. It was small and unmarked.

Her mother's words echoed in her mind.

This is my gift to you.

Taking a deep breath, Jane gathered the rest of the items and returned them to the box. She picked up the phone and placed it in the box alongside her other items and then thought better of it. Things had changed. She wasn't going to live her life in absolute fear of her husband. And, besides, she might need to make a call. Climbing up on the step stool, she placed the box back in the corner of the shelf. Before she could second guess herself, she dropped the phone in her purse, grabbed her car keys and headed out the door.

Jane only felt a slight tinge of guilt as she slid behind the wheel of her Mercedes. She checked the rearview mirror at least a dozen times as she pulled out of the building parking garage, certain she would see Devon's car pulling up behind her, but as she pulled out on the street everything around her was calm and quiet. She placed her hand on the navigation system in her car. She knew she couldn't just input the address on the paper into the system. Devon would most certainly check the history at some point. As her mother had told her, this was hers alone. She typed in "local library" and followed the directions to the nearest branch.

Inside, the librarian helped her sign in to a computer. Making sure no one was around, Jane typed in the address. Main Street Bank. It was not a bank she or her family had ever used, to the best of her knowledge.

Thinking quickly, Jane used her phone to call a cab. She wasn't sure if Devon could trace her in her car, but she wouldn't put it past him. She felt fiercely protective of her mother's last wishes and would do everything in her power to make sure the secret was not discovered.

The cab took her a short distance to the address she gave him, and she asked him to wait while she went inside.

She was greeted by a young man in a smart suit who asked if he could help her.

"Yes." She held up the key.

"Ah, you would like access to your safety deposit

box. Come this way, please."

Jane smiled and followed him to a separate part of the bank where he introduced her to a woman in a dark suit. "Ms. Jennings will help you with anything you need."

"Thank you."

Jane took a seat across from the woman.

"So, you want to access your safety deposit box?" The woman smiled pleasantly.

"Actually, my mother left it to me. I've not been here before," Jane explained.

"Okay, do you have an account number?" the woman asked, switching on her computer.

Jane handed over the piece of paper in her hand. "Is it one of these numbers?"

The lady took the sheet and began typing. After a moment she said, "Jane Bowen?"

"It's Jane Rawlings now."

The woman nodded. "I understand. A Miss Abagail Bowen left instructions that the contents of the box be left to her only daughter Jane Bowen or whatever married name her daughter may use. Is that you?"

Jane nodded.

"Do you have the key?"

Jane nodded again and held up the key.

The woman stood. "Okay, I'll need a copy of your ID, and then I will bring you the box."

Feeling her heart beat out of her chest, Jane complied with the request and then followed the woman into a small room. After several moments, the woman returned holding a rectangular metal box. She set it on the table in front of Jane and said, "Just let me know when you're done. Take all the time you need."

"Thank you."

Alone in the room, Jane felt the walls of the room start to close in on her. She had no idea of what lay inside the box. She wasn't sure how many more "surprises" her emotions could handle.

She sat for what seemed like an eternity staring at the solid metal box. Her hands remained frozen at her side.

"Oh, mother," she cried aloud. "I wish you were here."

I am here. It's okay.

A soft breeze wafted across Jane's body. She felt her tension release.

Her fingers curled around the box softly, caressing the hard metal frame.

Go ahead. Open it.

Feeling her mother's encouragement, Jane opened the lid to the box.

There was a large manila folder and a sealed rose-colored envelope, both with her name on them.

Jane immediately recognized her mother's personal stationary. She carefully opened the envelope and took out the handwritten letter.

My darling Jane –

If you are reading this, you have found my gift. I hope it reaches you in good spirits, but I fear that it doesn't.

I'm so sorry I have to leave you this way. I know that being a part of this family was never easy, but I'm afraid it will be even more difficult when I am gone. I wonder who will protect you – that has been my greatest responsibility so far. I know you are a strong girl and that you will take care of the family as I taught you, but

I also know that the responsibilities can be overwhelming.

At some time, your father will find a suitable husband for you. Suitable will mean someone like him. I have prayed you will be strong enough to resist the pattern of fear and submission, but, at the same time, I know that you don't know any other way. Please realize that you have choices. You have the right to live your life in any way you choose. Don't let anyone take that away from you.

In case the responsibilities become too much, I have put together a plan to help you. Your father doesn't know anything about this and, as such, your husband won't either. There is an attorney in town who is in charge of a trust set up for you. His information is attached. It's only a fraction of the inheritance that is rightfully yours, but if I'm correct, your husband controls that money. This is your parachute. While all of the money that was mine belongs to you ultimately, this is a small portion you may access and use immediately, without anyone knowing.

Be very careful if you decide to contact this attorney. If your father, or your husband, were to find out, there could be serious repercussions. I hope with all my heart that this small gift will help you in some way. It is my last effort to protect you from the legacy the women in our family have endured. I hope you will be strong enough to break the cycle.

Know that I am with you in spirit and that I will always take care of you.

Love

Mother

As she read, Jane could hear her mother's soft voice

floating in her ear. Of course, her mother had been in the same position she was in now. Her father had been essentially the same as Devon. They were both very powerful and very controlling. Although she had been loyal to her father to a fault, it had been a great deal of pressure to run his affairs, especially when she was younger. When she had married Devon, her father had hired a housekeeper, a cook, and two assistants to take her place. She, on the other hand, just transferred her responsibilities from one man to another.

I hope you will be strong enough to break the cycle.

Jane closed her eyes. Was that what her marriage entailed? Another link in an unbroken chain of suppression? Was that all she was to Devon? A housekeeper, cook, and assistant? She had thought she was his lover, but apparently, that was a job she shared with someone else.

A tremor of sorrow shook her body. She wanted to be more than that. She wanted to be, not just someone's lover, but the love of their life.

Setting down the delicate letter, Jane reached for the manila envelope. There was a copy of her mother's will, a document she was very familiar with. There were other documents that Jane had not seen before–including a power of attorney and a declaration of trust document. The last piece of paper included the name and address of a local attorney–presumably the one her mother had referenced in her letter.

John Blazier.

She had never heard the name before. Her father had certainly never mentioned it, and she couldn't recall ever hearing her mother talk about him either, although that was a long time ago when she had been fairly young.

Jane sat for a long time at the table in the small room to formulate a plan. A part of her felt as if things were spiraling out of her control, but at the same time, she felt like maybe things were actually falling right into place.

She didn't know how things would end with Devon. She couldn't go back to the way things were, but maybe there was still some hope for them. Maybe there wasn't.

Either way, Jane knew now that she had an out. She wasn't alone.

Her mother was with her.

The clerk at the back knocked on the door. "Can I get you anything?"

Jane called out as she picked up her phone. "I'm almost done. I just have to make one more phone call…"

Chapter Eleven

"Stephanie?"

Stephanie looked up from where she had been staring blankly at her phone. The last text message she had sent that said FOR A LONG TIME still blared on her screen.

Devon's wife had not replied.

Stephanie set down the phone and smiled at her secretary. "Yes?"

Kate held up an overflowing vase of flowers. "These just came for you."

"Oh." Stephanie was momentarily flustered. She couldn't remember the last time she received flowers for anything. Flower gifts were one of her pet peeves. They always died before one was finished enjoying them. It was easy to order flowers online. It was much harder to come up with something personal. Anyone who knew her knew not to send her flowers.

For a fleeting instant, she hoped maybe they were from Brad. He was the one person who didn't know that about her.

Kate set the arrangement on her desk. It was a lovely colorful bouquet full of day lilies, carnations, and tulips. Her assistant lingered, obviously hoping Stephanie would open the card in front of her, but Stephanie merely fingered the delicate flowers without making any move toward the attached card. Kate took the hint and scurried out of the office.

Once the door clicked into place, Stephanie raised a shaky hand to the small white envelope tucked inside the gorgeous arrangement. Her heart pounded in both excitement and trepidation.

The outside of the folded card read simply, "Thinking of you."

Slowly, Stephanie lifted the cover of the card.

And Missing You, DR

Stephanie closed the card and clenched it in her palm. They were from Devon. It was a risky move for him to send flowers to her office. One he would not normally even consider. He was clearly concerned about their relationship. But not concerned enough to take into account her personal preferences. The flowers weren't for her. He knew how she felt about them. They were to ease his guilt. He had often told her he would be lost without her, and that he didn't know what he would do if she weren't in his life. He said his life was cold and empty, and that she brought light into it.

Today, she was starting to doubt those words.

Stephanie ripped up the card into little pieces. She walked briskly across her office. Kate raised her head from her computer as Stephanie walked by, but Stephanie didn't stop to talk. She was on a mission.

Taking the elevator to the floor below, Stephanie walked through the massive cube farm housing the accounting department. In the large workroom, Stephanie buried the torn pieces of the card beside the other discarded paper remnants.

She grabbed a diet coke from the break room on her way out as an alibi and returned to her office.

As she passed by Kate's desk, she said, "The flowers

were from the Avery Family as a thank you for selling that land. Can you draft up a thank you note and put it on my desk? I want to hand deliver it."

Kate smiled. "Sure thing. They should be happy; you made them a nice little profit."

Stephanie nodded, trying her best to appear unfazed, and made her way back into her office. She removed the flowers from her desk, setting them on the credenza across the room. She didn't want Devon's guilty offerings anywhere near her.

Immediately after she sat down in her chair, her cell phone rang. She jumped and looked at the screen. It was Devon. She wondered how many times he had called while she was out. She knew if she didn't answer, he would continue to call until her entire day was disrupted. And on top of it all, she knew he would expect her to gush over his thoughtfulness in sending flowers that she couldn't talk about to her workplace, also disrupting her entire day.

Feeling annoyed, she hit the CALL button, "Hey." No sense in pretending she didn't know who it was.

"Hey what?" he prompted, and she knew exactly what he referred to. Their private greeting. Feeling a weight descend on her chest, she amended, "Hey, you."

"Hey yourself."

Stephanie cringed at the deep, conspiratorial tone of his voice. She had always thought it sounded so romantic. Now, it just sounded creepy.

"Thank you for the flowers," she said, cutting to the chase.

"I just wanted to say I'm sorry for last night. I was just worried, that's all." She could hear the desperation in his voice. For once, it didn't sway her.

"You don't need to worry about me." She was a grown woman, after all. She was getting tired of playing the game.

There was a pause.

"I do worry. I care about you."

Right. Although she wasn't sure his definition of caring matched hers any longer. Still, she was at work and not in a position to start an argument. What she really wanted was to get off the phone. Lowering her voice, she replied, "I know."

"Do you want me to come over tonight?"

NO, her inner mind screamed.

Stephanie stood up and began pacing her office restlessly. How had things gotten so out of control so quickly? She felt like a caged animal being held captive in a relationship she didn't have any control over. The relationship had always been a one-way road and now she realized it was also a dead end. Devon didn't love her. He loved to control her. And she allowed it to happen. Stephanie didn't blame him. She blamed herself. She should have been strong enough to end things a long time ago before Devon became so obsessed. But now, she didn't know what would happen if she tried to end it.

To her or to Devon's wife.

"I have a client meeting," she improvised in answer to his question. "Why don't you call me later when you're available?"

His tone grew clipped. "What kind of client meeting would you have at night?"

Visions of Devon showing up at her office filled her head. For the first time, she realized what a dangerous position she had put herself in.

"I didn't mean tonight," she backtracked. "But late

in the afternoon. I'm not sure how long it will take. And then I was going to go for a run afterward."

Putting himself back on the offensive, he replied, "Maybe I will stop by later tonight. If I do, I hope you will be home."

The threat in his voice came through loud and clear. He expected her to rush home and wait for him all evening. It would right the power levels again. And, not so long ago, that is exactly what would have happened. In fact, Stephanie probably wouldn't have thought twice about it. She would have run home, showered, changed into something sexy, and waited. If he showed up, it would have been a wonderful half hour or hour, and then, ultimately, she would have gone to bed alone. If not, she would have gone to bed alone and disappointed. Either way, she went to bed alone.

Stephanie disconnected the phone and sank back into her chair, exhausted. Her forehead was covered with beads of perspiration and her hands felt clammy. Reaching for her purse, she quickly applied a layer of powder to her face and a touch of lipstick. No matter how tumultuous her insides felt, she needed to present a composed façade to her colleagues.

"Hey, you."

Stephanie physically jumped at the familiar greeting. It startled her so much she knocked a picture frame from her desk. Her heart pounded wildly, and she gasped for breath even as she grabbed for the wayward picture in hopes of saving it from hitting the ground.

Brad rushed forward to retrieve the wayward photo. "I'm sorry."

"Oh, no," Stephanie felt flustered as she gathered her composure. For an instant, she had heard Devon's voice in the words being spoken, even though Brad stood before her smiling his sweet, boyish smile. "You just… I just…" She took a deep breath, placed her hands on her desk, and looked up at Brad with a smile. "Hi."

He grinned back. "I didn't mean to scare you."

Stephanie shook her head in dismissal of the apology. "You didn't. I was just thinking about something else."

"Something important? Anything I can do to help?" He sat down in one of the guest chairs facing her desk. His expression was earnest. His offer had been completely sincere. She had no doubt in her mind that whatever Stephanie shared with him, he would do his best to help her. He was a genuine person who cared about other people. It was refreshing.

But her current situation was one she would have to deal with on her own. She knew that as well.

She shook her head. "No, it wasn't anything important."

"Hey, if it's important to you, it's important to me, so just say the word and I'll help you out. Not that you need my help… But, if you did…" Brad stopped and grinned at her. "I'm rambling. I know. I do that, by the way, a lot." She laughed, and he changed the subject. "I wanted to come by earlier, but I had a stupid budget meeting that lasted all morning. I know there's like a rule and all about being cool, but I wanted to tell you what a great time I had with you last night. I mean, like, a really, really good time…" He held up a hand. "I know, rambling again."

She felt her skin blush and softened her smile. Had it really been just one night? It seemed her entire world had turned upside down in the course of the past day.

Just five minutes with Brad had eased the tension from her shoulders. He was so easy to like. "I had a good time as well."

"Do you want to do it again tonight? I know there's a rule about waiting three days or whatever, but…"

Stephanie laughed out loud. But then she turned serious. "I can't tonight."

"Oh." Brad's smile faded. "Do you hate me? Because if you do just tell me…"

Stephanie stood up and walked around her desk, taking the second guest chair facing Brad. She took his hands in hers. They were warm and soft and full of strength. "No, I don't hate you. In fact, it's because I like you, that I can't have dinner."

"Not following," Brad said with a look of concern showing on his face.

"I have some things I need to take care of."

"Boyfriend things?"

Stephanie shook her head. There was no way she was going to refer to Devon as her 'boyfriend.' "Not exactly. But, personal. And I know there's a rule about saying things like this at this point in a relationship, but I really like you."

"There is no rule against that," Brad said, smiling at her. "I like you too." His voice was calm and self-assured, and she had no doubt they were sincere.

"Well, then I'm pretty sure there is a rule against saying this…" She looked into his clear brown eyes and felt herself get a little lost in them. They were warm and inviting, not cold and intimidating. The kind of eyes she wanted to stare into forever.

He squeezed her hand in a gesture of support, and she nodded, steeling herself for the words she was about to utter. "Okay, well, I know its early, and we are still getting to know each other, but I've never felt this way before, and I..." she stopped and took a deep breath, "...well, I think we could be great together."

She closed her eyes for a moment as the words filled the air like a thick cloud. She couldn't believe she said the words, but, by God, she didn't want to lose this light shining in front of her, and she couldn't run to him until she got rid of the baggage she had been carrying for far too long.

When she opened her eyes, Brad was staring at her silently, and she couldn't read his expression, but she had come this far, she wasn't going to back down now. "And because I feel so strongly about what we could be, I want to take care of some things before this gets any more serious."

Brad watched her for a moment. In her mind, she sounded unstable, even to herself. Who admitted something like that after just one day? It was crazy. But it was true. And she wasn't going to take it back. And she wasn't done. "I know it sounds ridiculous, but it is important to me. I want our relationship to start perfectly clean. I want to be able to take it wherever it goes and not have anything hanging over my shoulder. I feel that strongly about what we might have together."

STOP, her inner voice silently screamed. If she didn't stop herself right now, she would be showing him pictures of wedding dresses.

"Wow," Brad whispered.

"What?" Stephanie stopped and stared. It was too much. She had scared him off.

"You ramble when you're nervous, too."

"No, I don't," Stephanie protested and then realized

that of course she had been rambling. She blushed and stammered, "Only when I'm trying not to sound completely insane."

She started to regret her spontaneous outburst.

Brad smiled at her. "Actually, that was probably the nicest thing anyone has ever said to me."

"Really?" Stephanie sank down into her chair.

"Yes, really." Brad's voice sounded soft and sexy, and Stephanie allowed herself to look at him fully in the face. His expression was so beautiful. He smiled at her.

To her horror, Stephanie felt tears well up in her eyes. Oh, God, now she was going to cry. Again. What was happening?

He either didn't notice, or pretended not to, which was perfectly gentleman-like on its own. Instead he said, "Take all the time you need." Then he shook his head, amending, "I mean, not too much time because I'm not getting any younger, you know, but, really, all the time you need…"

He grinned, and she laughed.

"Seriously," he said, "I couldn't be more flattered, and I definitely think you are worth waiting for. You tell me whenever you are ready. And besides, having dinner surely doesn't mean we can't have lunch, or coffee, or even take in a matinee, right?"

Stephanie laughed again. "I think that all sounds perfect."

"Great." Brad stood to leave her office and noticed the flowers. "Beautiful flowers." He turned back to her. "You know, for some reason, I wouldn't take you as a flower person."

Stephanie couldn't contain the smile on her face. "I hate flowers."

Brad laughed. "I'll keep that in mind."

And Stephanie knew that he would.

With a smile, she picked up the document on her desk and started to read. She hadn't passed the first paragraph when her phone vibrated.

Her shoulders slumped. How did Devon always know when she was experiencing a sliver of happiness?

She looked down, but instead of Devon's phone number, there was a new text.

DO YOU LOVE HIM?

With everything else that had gone on this afternoon, Stephanie had forgotten about her text conversation with his wife. Had that really only been hours ago?

She stared at the words for a long moment. There was a time when she would not have thought twice about the answer. Devon had been her world for a very long time. But, in just the short time she had known Brad, she realized love wasn't ten minutes on the phone or a stolen evening once a week. Sure, Devon said all the right things, and there was definitely a connection between them, but there was no future. That wasn't love. It was an obsession.

The truth was - she owed it to this woman, and to herself, to be honest.

I DID.

She waited to see what kind of response she would get. She got the feeling his wife wasn't as fragile as Devon had led her to believe. The incoming response was further proof of that.

SO DID I.

Stephanie was surprised at the simple statement. What did she mean did? If they didn't love each other, why were they still together?

I'M NOT SURE I UNDERSTAND, she typed. She was under the impression Devon's wife was dependent on him. It was why they were still together. How many times had she been told that? Too many to count.

HE WON'T LEAVE ME.

Stephanie nodded her head. She understood the statement completely. They were being completely honest, certainly an easier task over an intangible object than it ever could be in person.

I KNOW. HE WANTS TO TAKE CARE OF YOU.

There was a pause.

THAT'S NOT IT.

Stephanie felt a chill run up her spine.

WHAT DO YOU MEAN?

The text beeped instantly.

HE WANTS TO CONTROL ME.

Stephanie flinched at the harsh tone. She knew Devon had a strong personality, but she had always presumed he was softer with his wife – given her fragile state. He made it seem that her well-being meant so much to him. After all, he provided her a very comfortable lifestyle. There was nothing she didn't have. It had caused Stephanie many jealous moments. Maybe his wife didn't see how Devon showed his love by taking caring of her. Either way, one of them was wrong. Stephanie didn't want to insult the woman and possibly push her away.

I THINK HE WANTS TO PROVIDE YOU THE COMFORTABLE LIFESTYLE THAT YOU ARE USED TO.

There was a longer pause.

THE MONEY IS MINE.

The words shattered in Stephanie's brain. In a matter of four short words, everything Stephanie had been led to believe crumbled into ashes. Her entire relationship with Devon had centered around the fact that he couldn't leave his wife. That was probably true, but not because of a sense of duty to her. It was because she had the money. He didn't want to leave her money.

Stephanie felt an anger rage through her. How stupid could she have been? She had wasted so much time on something that was so hurtful and full of lies.

A knock on the door startled her out of her trance.

She looked up just as Brad poked his head in the door. Stephanie switched off her phone and dropped it in her purse.

"Back so soon?" she asked, trying to compose her twisted insides into some semblance of calm.

Brad smiled at her and crossed the room.

"Come have coffee," Brad suggested, standing at the edge of her desk. "As coworkers." Despite the fact she hadn't gotten any work done all afternoon, Stephanie shrugged and said, "Sure."

They walked amicably two blocks over to the local coffee shop. Late in the afternoon, it was brimming with students working on laptops and businessmen reading over contracts or other documents. They found a quiet table in the back, and Brad brought two large coffees and a chocolate chip cookie.

"There wasn't much of a selection," he confided, setting the cookie down on the table between them.

Stephanie broke off a small piece and popped it into her mouth. "Chocolate chip is my favorite."

Brad leaned forward, "So, let's take it slow. Tell me everything about you…" He laughed.

Three hours later, Stephanie pulled into the driveway of her house. It was well after 7:00PM. She and Brad had found so much to talk about that the time flew by. As it was, she hated to leave Brad – she had never felt so comfortable with someone in her whole life. Although it had been only a short time, she felt as if she had known him forever. For the first time in her life, she actually thought she might believe in the words soul mate. They had shared a kiss good night in which Brad was respectful of her desire to move slowly, but she certainly could see a glimpse of the passion that lay just underneath.

As she turned off the engine, she was thankful her driveway was empty. The windows of her house were dark. She didn't want to face Devon this evening. Just being with Brad highlighted how dysfunctional her relationship with Devon was. Despite the obvious, it wasn't healthy to be with someone who needed so much control. Even if things ultimately didn't work out with Brad, Stephanie had concluded it was time to end her relationship with Devon. For good.

Stephanie got out of the car and walked around the passenger door to retrieve her purse and briefcase. As she rounded the front of the door, she stepped on an empty soda can in the driveway. She stooped and picked it up, carrying it to the trash bin at the top of the drive. When she got there, she noticed the lid was up on her bin. Scattered around were pieces of her trash. A prickle ran up her spine.

She looked around, but her surroundings were quiet. Had a raccoon or cat gotten into the trash? She supposed it was possible, likely even; but the idea that an animal would be able to climb up the can, lift the lid and dig through the bin without knocking it over seemed a little far-fetched. It looked like, to her, someone had rifled through her trash.

Stephanie peered inside the bin. Soda can, toilet paper roll, junk mail... There was nothing valuable, or even exciting, inside. She was careful to shred her bills and other mail, so she wasn't worried about identity theft. She gave a shrug and pulled the lid closed. She was pretty certain that whatever someone was looking for, they didn't find.

Still, as she entered her home, she was careful to check all the locks on the doors and windows and pulled her blinds closed as she prepared for her evening.

Devon never called.

Chapter Twelve

I'M LEAVING HIM.

The message had been sent three days ago – after Jane had revealed that the money was hers.

Jane didn't respond immediately. In some ways, it felt like someone else's problem. She felt so detached she couldn't even muster the energy to be relieved.

Truth was, she wasn't relieved. She was afraid.

She was afraid of what Devon would do, to this woman and to her, if either one of them left him.

This woman she didn't even know was tied to her in a way she could not have even imagined. And she couldn't escape it. Not any longer.

Jane felt angry.

Jane felt betrayed.

And Jane felt responsible.

With a deep sigh, she picked up her phone. She stared at it for a long while and then typed.

IS EVERYTHING OKAY?

The woman must have had her phone out for the text icon popped up immediately.

YES. HOW ABOUT YOU?

Jane shrugged a shoulder to herself. She wasn't about to reveal to anyone, especially this woman, her own plans. Her goal now was to protect herself. She typed:

THE SAME. HAVE YOU LEFT HIM YET?

It was a little blunt, but Jane was curious. She didn't think so because Devon had been actually fairly normal over the past few days, but she wanted to know for sure.

NO. I DON'T KNOW HOW.

Jane smiled tightly. Of course, she didn't. There was no easy way to leave Devon Rawlings. She wasn't sure there was any way at all.

YOU'LL HAVE TO BE CAREFUL.

There was a slight pause and then.

WILL HE HURT YOU IF I LEAVE HIM?

Jane's smile turned to a hard laugh. In some ways, Jane felt a thousand years old. She had been through too much. Her illusions were already shattered. This woman was still naïve. She thought things would end well for her. Jane's fingers flew over the keypad.

YES. BUT I'M NOT AFRAID OF THAT.

WHAT ARE YOU AFRAID OF?

Jane didn't hesitate.

I'M AFRAID THAT HE WILL HURT YOU.

****

Stephanie's hands shook uncontrollably as she read the words on her screen. How had she climbed into this nightmare? Devon was her soul mate. The love of her life. He would never hurt her.

Stephanie shook her head.

No.

The nagging voice that had always had a place in the recesses of her heart, started to yell.

It was a lie. It had always been a lie.

And now, she relied on the one person who should hate her the most to help her out of the hell she had fallen into.

WHAT SHOULD I DO?

There was a long pause. Stephanie couldn't be upset if the woman chose not to answer. After all, Stephanie was the home-wrecker. She didn't owe Stephanie a thing. Not a damn thing.

LEAVE THE CITY. AT LEAST FOR A WHILE .

Stephanie stared at the words on her screen. Leave the city? How could she even manage that? She had a job. And a life. And Brad…

Her relationship with Brad was like a beacon guiding her out of the darkness. The more time she spent with him, innocent as it was, the more she realized how toxic her relationship with Devon was. And always had been. She took such pride in all of her accomplishments, in her independence, and yet, she was the very description of co-dependent. She relied on Devon for approval. She allowed him to control her own measure of self-worth. It made her sick, to think about it now.

With Brad, though, she knew she had a real chance at happiness. She desperately wished she could face Brad and say, in all honestly, I'm free to love you. But she wasn't free. And she wasn't sure that even if she was, Brad could forgive her. All the stereotypes associated with being a mistress or a home-wrecker crashed down on her soul. Maybe Brad would see her as tainted. It was how she saw herself.

And, even worse, she had to consider, not only Brad, but this woman, his wife. She almost felt the tension in the other woman's words. There was no mistaking the severity of the situation. Devon would hurt both of them if either one dared to leave.

The safety of each one of them hung in the balance of her decision. Someone she should never have encountered was a part of this wicked web of lies and deception. How could she risk the safety of another human being? Her freedom could very well cost someone else their life.

Stephanie closed her eyes, feeling the gravity of her situation weighing down her very soul. She asked the one question she feared the most.

WHAT ABOUT YOU?

Stephanie couldn't let this woman, the woman she had considered her enemy for so long, bear the brunt of her evil.

I CAN TAKE CARE OF MYSELF.

Chapter Thirteen

"You're awful quiet tonight," Devon remarked at dinner.

Jane placed a forkful of roasted potato in her mouth. She wasn't being any different than any other night, and Devon knew it. In the two weeks that had passed since the broken lamp incident, Devon's mood swung from vulnerable to edgy on a whim. It was like he wanted to be aggressive, but would force himself to hold back. And tonight, as usual, he was just trying to get a rise out of her.

Every day, Jane had gone to great efforts to make sure that everything was in order. The house was in pristine condition. Dinner had been perfectly prepared hot on the table when Devon arrived home from work. Tonight, Jane, always perfectly coiffed and made up, wore a simple cashmere sweater and jeans. On the outside, she behaved exactly the same as any other time. On the inside; however, nothing was the same.

In response to his comment, she merely smiled and asked, "What would you like to know?" Devon knew good and well that she never started a conversation with him unless he asked her to. She was not behaving one iota differently than any other night. He was baiting her. This time, she refused to fall for it.

Devon set down his fork and stared hard at her. She could see he wanted to get angry with her but restrained himself. Things must be going really poorly with his lover. She had been texting Stephanie occasionally and got the distinct impression that the other woman was serious about looking for a way out of the relationship. Served him right. Jane smiled again.

Devon narrowed his eyes and went straight for the punch. "I noticed you took the car out again today."

Jane kept the smile pasted on her face. Even though she had expected it at some point, it was still shocking to realize he was checking her parking space. She wondered what else he checked. She had been so careful of her moves recently she was certain she had covered her tracks on everything, but she knew better than to take Devon˙ for granted. He was manipulative and had unlimited resources. At least for now.

Jane worked to calm her nerves. She couldn't panic now. So, he had noticed her car had been moved. Fine. She had prepared for that.

Nodding, she replied calmly, "I did. I had a yoga class earlier today."

It was true. She had purposely planned her recent excursions around the yoga schedule. Today, she had met with her attorney at a local coffee shop hidden behind the yoga studio. When she left the coffee shop, she had gone straight to her morning yoga class. If he checked, she had been there the entire class.

"Why didn't you have George drive you?" She could hear the edge in his voice. He didn't like her doing things on her own.

Well, he didn't make all the rules anymore.

Jane met his gaze. His eyes were dark. Inside, her heart started to pound a little harder. She was treading on dangerous ground now. Jane might have had an epiphany about life, but Devon didn't know that. She might be stronger emotionally, but she was still no match for his physical strength. She was banking on his current vulnerability, but there was no guarantee that it would last.

With a deep breath, she said evenly, but with a firm tone, "I don't need George to drive me. I have a car and a license. It's silly. I can drive myself to yoga from now on."

"Oh, you can drive yourself to yoga from now on, can you?" Devon mocked her.

Jane closed her eyes. She would not be intimidated. "Devon, it's just yoga. You are welcome to come with me, but I will drive myself. Don't make it a bigger deal than it is."

She kept her voice soft and steady, but she couldn't remember the last time she had stood up for herself in such a fashion to her husband, even delivered in a soft tone.

Devon opened his mouth to answer. His eyes grew narrow. Jane met his gaze. She couldn't control his response. If he was going to hit her, there wasn't anything she could do to prevent it. She knew that now. He must have seen the resolve in her face because he closed his mouth without responding.

Picking up his fork, he took a bite of the pork tenderloin on his plate. Then he took a sip of wine. When he met her gaze once more, his eyes were clear. "I just worry about you, that's all."

She could see the vulnerability on his face. At one time that would have melted her heart. But, tonight, it just repulsed her. With a small smile, she picked up her water glass and said, "I know."

After dinner, as Jane finished up the last of the dishes, she remarked, trying to keep the smugness out of her voice. "Were you planning to go back to the office this evening?"

It wasn't unusual for Devon to leave in the evening; only now Jane knew exactly what that meant. Lately, he had been leaving the house fewer and fewer times. On the rare occasion that he did go, she had a fleeting notion to follow him but knew instinctively it was too dangerous. Devon was not a stupid man. He would not be easily fooled.

In her heart, she knew what was happening. His lover was distancing herself from him. Trying to break free. The woman had not taken her advice and just left town. There was no easy way to let Devon down gently. He would never let either one of them go without a fight. He didn't like to lose.

But until then, he felt vulnerable. Jane had no illusions–that vulnerability had nothing to do with her and everything to do with the woman he cheated on her with.

She was probably making excuses, like a sick relative or work travel, to avoid seeing him. It would work for a short period, but Devon's patience would wear thin.

Jane dreaded the day that happened.

As he stayed in more and more, he spent more time in his office. Brooding, probably. Or lining up his next conquest. Jane now understood Devon would never be faithful to her. She would never be enough for him. Still, as his mistress seemingly pulled away, he clung harder to her.

There was a long pause as presumably Devon

considered her comment. After a long moment, he declared, "I've decided not to go out tonight."

Ah, rejected again, Jane thought. This time she was unable to suppress her smile before Devon caught a glimpse of it.

"Is something funny?" His voice turned cold, and Jane quickly rearranged her face to be void of any emotion.

"Of course not. I'm happy to have you home for the evening."

He narrowed his gaze and took a step in her direction. "It certainly doesn't seem like it to me."

Jane took a step back and turned away, clearing the dinner dishes and putting them in the sink to avoid having to face him. It looked like tonight, despite all of her efforts, he was spoiling for a fight. She sighed and replied, "I'm sorry it doesn't look that way to you."

"Look at me when you talk to me." He grabbed her arm and spun her around, causing her to drop the plate she held in her hand. On impulse, she yanked her arm out of his grip.

He raised the palm of his hand and brought it down against her cheek, knocking her down to one knee. She tasted blood inside her cheek. She looked up at him, letting the hate show in her eyes.

He yanked her to her feet by her hair. His face was distorted with rage. She knew he was no longer thinking clearly. "Who do you think you are? How dare you disrespect me?" He dragged her into the living room and threw her down on the sofa. She hit her hip hard against the arm rest.

"I think I'm your wife," she said, blood spilling over her lips.

"No." he spat. "My WIFE," he emphasized the word, "would never go off against my wishes. Do you think I don't know what you are up to? Sneaking out in the middle of the day? Doing God knows what. You are nothing more than a cheap slut. You probably take your clothes off for anyone who walks by."

"No, Devon," she pleaded, trying not to whimper as he moved toward her. "That's not true. You are the only man I've ever been with. You know that."

He reached down and tore open the front of her shirt. He fondled her breasts, but his grip was hard and painful. Her heart pounded in her chest, but she would not back down. She had endured worse. He squeezed her nipples until she grimaced in pain. He lowered his voice so that it was deep and seductive, yet his tone remained cruel and mocking, "I don't know that at all. You showed me a different side the other night. Where did you learn that? Who taught you that?"

"You taught me that, Devon. You made me what I am," she cried.

"That's right," he answered, his face so close to hers she could see the spittle on his upper lip. "I made you. No, I take that back. I bought you. Your daddy made you."

Jane closed her eyes to avoid the fury staring back at her, but Devon continued talking. "Your daddy raised himself the perfect little girl. And then he gave her to me. And he taught me exactly what to do with her. The same things he did with your mother."

Each word hit like a hammer to Jane's soul.

Devon pulled her into a sitting position. He stood before her and slowly undid his belt.

"I own you, Jane. And if you try to fight me, so help

me God, anything I've done in the past will seem like child's play compared to what I will do to you then. Do you understand?"

With his hands tangled in her hair, he forced her to nod. He put his face against hers and in a quiet voice that left absolutely no room for doubt, he added, "Let me be perfectly clear. You are my wife. You belong to me. If you ever go against me, I will kill you."

She knew Devon liked to see fear in her eyes, and she didn't have to pretend. She had seen her husband be cruel and hurtful before, but this was different. There was something savage in his behavior like he was losing whatever grip he had on sanity.

She was afraid she would pay the ultimate price.

Devon roughly lifted her hands. He wrapped the belt loop around them and pulled it tight. Her hands immediately tingled as circulation was removed. He grabbed the belt and dragged her from the sofa onto the floor, where she lay flat, unable to protect or cover herself.

He towered over her, staring down at her prone body.

She was exposed and vulnerable.

"Are you afraid?" he taunted, looking at her with disdain.

Jane swallowed. Truthfully, she was afraid, but she'd be damned if she was going to admit it out loud. He was going to do whatever he wanted to her anyway. It didn't matter what she said.

When she remained silent, Devon scowled. He pulled his foot back and kicked her in the ribs with all of his might. Jane, taken by surprise, grunted as a white-hot flash seared her side. The force of the kick actually moved her body across the floor and sucked the breath right out of her.

He laughed at the sight of her surprise. "You've gotten complacent. You think I want to fuck you? You're a whore. No, it's time you learned a different lesson."

He lifted his foot to kick her again, but she rolled out of the way. True terror rose in her gut. Was this the night? Was this the night he was going to kill her?

She managed to raise herself enough to scoot with her knees along the floor away from him. He grabbed her by the thigh and pulled her back to the floor. His grip grew so tight she could feel the skin bruise beneath his fingers.

She strained her fingers over her head, trying to grab the leg of the coffee table or the sofa or anything for stability so she could somehow protect herself.

He cupped her cheek softly. The gentleness of his touch was a sharp contrast to the ice in his eyes. "You have such smooth skin. Such a delicate pale shade." He caressed her. "Like porcelain." He pulled back his hand and slapped her across the face. She felt the sting of his fingers like fire across his skin. He laughed. "Such a perfect imprint of my hand."

Jane felt stars dancing above her eyes from the force of his slap. He had never hit her in the face before. The pain was almost unbearable. She thought she might pass out and struggled to remain alert. She was truly afraid of what he would do if she was completely unable to defend herself. It felt to her as if he'd lost touch with reality.

He raised his hand to strike her again, and Jane braced herself from the blow. She knew she wouldn't be able to take much more. She would have to escape to her happy place and then there was no telling what he would do.

On the coffee table next to them, Devon's phone vibrated.

The interruption startled both of them.

Devon stopped and stared at his phone, as if wondering how it got there.

Jane didn't care how it got there, she was thankful for the reprieve.

Slowly, Devon picked it up, looking at the screen.

He shook his head in mock disappointment. "I'm afraid I have to take this."

Jane managed to get herself into a seating position, but she was still completely exposed. Devon yanked the belt from her hands, which were completely numb. She allowed them to drop to her side. She was afraid to make any kind of movement. She did want to attract his attention any further.

Devon spoke briefly into the phone and then said, "Yes, hold on a moment."

He put his phone on mute and leaned down to where Jane lay. "I have to take this call. We will have to continue our lesson another time."

Jane didn't move. Didn't respond.

Devon started for his office and then turned back to her, leaning his face close to hers. "By the way, we are going to a party on Friday. Don't make other plans."

Still groggy from the attack, Jane asked, "What kind of party?"

Devon reached for her chin and pulled her face to meet his gaze. "The kind of party where you are going to stand there and look pretty and do whatever I say. Do you understand?"

Jane nodded, and Devon released his grip, turning

his back to her. Putting the phone to his ear, Devon walked to his office and shut the door.

As soon as she heard the lock turn, Jane jumped up and ran up the stairs to the bedroom. Once inside, she slammed the door and turned the lock. She had never, not once, locked the door to any room in the house, but she didn't give a damn tonight.

Falling across the bed, she closed her eyes and allowed the pain from the evening to settle into a dull thumping throughout her body. She was fairly certain she had a broken rib and her body, the non-visible parts anyway, would be bruised by morning.

After all these years, the gloves were off. There was no more denying it. Devon had admitted that she was an object to him. As he himself said, he had bought her. She was his possession.

In spite of her mother's precautions, there wasn't enough to save Jane from suffering the same fate. Jane was as trapped as her mother had ever been.

There was no way out.

At least no easy way.

Chapter Fourteen

"You look fabulous," Brad gushed as Stephanie stepped from her bedroom into the living room. She wore a royal blue strapless gown. It brought out the blue in her eyes. It was sophisticated and feminine, and Stephanie felt like royalty in it. Brad had helped her pick it out last week. Despite her best efforts, keeping him at arm's length had been impossible. She still hadn't worked things out with Devon, but she couldn't deny the attraction for Brad and found it harder and harder to stay away from him. Coffee had turned into lunch, which had turned into dinner, and now, even the occasional visit to her apartment. Every time he came over though, Stephanie panicked Devon would show up unannounced. It was like a dead weight she carried around with her everywhere and it was really wearing on her.

"You okay?" Brad asked, seeing the shadow cross over her face.

Stephanie both loved and hated that Brad could read her so well. He was so in tune with her that he took the time to notice changes in her expression or mannerisms. He was always concerned about her well-being and happiness. That she loved.

She hated that so much of her time was spent being guarded and tense. She had broken down and told Brad a portion of her situation. That she was having difficulty breaking up with an ex-boyfriend. She didn't mention the part about him being married. She just couldn't force herself to say it out loud. It sounded so much worse than she had thought. Because she was afraid for her safety and potentially his as well, she had told him her ex-boyfriend was extremely jealous and potentially unstable. She knew women probably said that all the time, but in her case it was true. Brad had offered to talk to him for her, and Stephanie had quickly squashed the idea. There was no telling what Devon would do if he knew about Brad.

Through it all, Brad had been nothing but supportive. She had been as honest with him as possible and he understood. Even though he knew there were ghosts in her closet, he wanted to be with her and did his best to support her decisions.

Devon, on the other hand, was another problem. She had been making excuses for weeks to avoid seeing him, forced to be more and more obvious. She knew she would be forced to have a face-to-face confrontation at some point, but she was petrified of his reaction. For now, it was easier to avoid the situation completely.

Pushing thoughts of Devon aside, she smiled back at Brad. "I'm fine." Then she fingered her elaborate updo nervously. "Do you think it's too much?" The hairdresser had opted for a loose twist with wavy tendrils framing her face. She said it showed off Stephanie's collarbone to perfection, but Stephanie worried it showed too much expanse of skin at her neckline.

Brad shook his head. "Are you kidding? It's perfect. After all, you are winning the real estate attorney of the year award."

"I know, but, it's a professional event. With my hair

like this, my shoulders are completely exposed." She rubbed her hands over her bare arms. "Maybe I should wear a jacket."

Brad placed his hands on top of hers. "Honey, you don't need a jacket. You look gorgeous and elegant just the way you are." He placed a series of feather kisses along her shoulder bone. "You are perfect."

Stephanie shivered as the soft kisses sent chills down her spine and said, "You're being very sweet."

"I'm being honest," he whispered and pulled her into his arms, kissing her on the lips. Unlike Devon, whose kisses were always demanding and urgent, kissing Brad felt like wrapping herself in a warm, soft comforter. He was gentle and considerate but left no mistake that he was all man. His arms were strong as he wrapped them around her. He was a confident lover, but not arrogant, and Stephanie quickly discovered what a big difference there was between the two.

She savored his kisses for a long moment and then sighed audibly. "We have to go."

Groaning, Brad pulled away. "I know. It wouldn't do to have the attorney of the year showing up late for the awards ceremony."

He offered her his arm. "Come, my dear. Your audience awaits."

****

"Get a move on, we have to go," Devon bellowed up the stairs.

Jane cringed as his angry voice reached her ears and turned toward the full-length mirror in distress. How could she go out in public like this?

This morning, Devon had tossed a garment bag across the bed, saying casually, "Here is your dress for tonight."

Since Devon purchased all of her formal dresses, she hadn't thought twice about it all day. She had gone about her household duties until just before Devon arrived home when she started dressing. And now, here she was, showered and made up, wearing what could only be the equivalent of a nightgown.

She fought tears of shame. The dress was a thin silk material with rhinestone straps. The dress was not lined and clung to every curve. It was absolutely not appropriate for anything but the bedroom.

She knew Devon was baiting her. He had been unbearable for the past week, constantly berating her and deliberately creating situations for her to clean up or take care of. She was doing her best not to be intimidated, but she was afraid his vengeance was spiraling out of control. He also watched her constantly, and she had a strong suspicion someone was following her. She hadn't had the nerve to visit her attorney at all this week but, thanks to her cell phone, which she guarded with dear life, she had given him certain instructions. She constantly walked a tightrope, and she felt as if she might fall at any moment.

She risked one last glance in the mirror. Her face and hair looked perfect–soft and subtle, but one downward movement of the eye, and she immediately noticed that the outline of her nipples was clearly visible through the thin fabric of her dress.

She closed her eyes and moved toward the bedroom door. Devon waited for her at the bottom of the stairs. He watched her descend with an evil gleam in his eyes. "Do you like the dress I picked for you?" he sneered as she approached.

"Are you sure this is what you want me to wear?" she asked. She just couldn't believe that, no matter how much he wanted to humiliate her, he would actually allow her to accompany him to a professional event in this outfit. His professional reputation was everything to him. She expected at any moment for him to demand she change into something more appropriate.

Instead, he smiled. "Absolutely. If you are going to act like a tramp, you might as well dress like one."

Even though he had been having an affair for God knows how long, he had stuck with the notion that she somehow had committed infidelities. It was a ridiculous idea, but it seemed somehow to give him pleasure to needle her about it tirelessly.

She knew better than to argue further. With a deep sigh, she responded, "Fine," and reached for her purse.

Jane still didn't know what event they were attending. She had been relieved of her scheduling duties–for that event anyway. To be honest, she no longer really cared. Jane had more important concerns– like maintaining her safety. Her body still had bruises internally from last week's beating, and she had gone out of her way to try and avoid any further confrontations. Devon must have been planning this little humiliation all week because he was careful to only abuse her verbally– he clearly wanted to make sure that the vast amount of skin that he planned to force her to show tonight appeared smooth and unblemished.

They took Devon's Mercedes across town to a warehouse on the outskirts of downtown. The billboard out front stated that the building was scheduled for redevelopment into high-end condos. Jane looked at Devon in confusion. Was Devon investing in the property? She couldn't for the life of her imagine what they were doing here.

"Is this a hospital event?" she asked quietly.

"No."

That was all. No further explanation.

Devon got out of the car and walked to the front entrance which had a red carpet and velvet ropes, leaving Jane sitting alone in the passenger seat. With an apologetic look, the valet attendant came to her side and assisted her exit from the car. Jane had to rush to catch up with her husband as he entered the venue. He didn't offer a backwards glance.

Once inside, Jane stood awkwardly as Devon scouted the room. Not one face was recognizable to her and the banner on the wall was the name of a local law firm. As far as she knew, it wasn't a firm Devon used, and, to her relief, she had no connection either. So why were they here?

"Get me a drink," Devon ordered, not even glancing in her direction.

Jane did as she was told. Normally, she would have bristled at his attitude, but she was eager to have something to do. She felt exposed and uncomfortable just standing around.

As she made her way to the bar, she noticed men's eyes falling onto her exposed chest. She couldn't even fault them for it. After all, if she showed up and put it out there, she could hardly blame anyone for noticing. Still, she knew her face was beet red as she subtly placed her hands over her chest area. Even so, her figure was blatantly revealed in the clingy dress.

"Can I get you a drink?"

A tall man in a black suit standing in line in front of

her gave her a suggestive smile as he made the offer.

Jane blushed even redder and quickly shook her head. "No, thank you."

The man shrugged, took his drink, and walked away.

Jane stepped up to the bar and placed her order.

"Let me get that for you," another man quickly suggested, rushing to stand beside her.

"No, thank you," she repeated with an exasperated edge to her voice and gave the bartender her order.

"Come on, it's just a drink," the guy persisted. He moved in to stand too close to her, and she took a step away.

"It's for my husband," she replied sharply, giving the man a warning look.

He took a step backward, but looked around as if to say, "I don't see anyone."

Jane followed his gaze and sure enough, Devon was nowhere to be seen.

The man raised his eyebrows in her direction, as if waiting for an explanation.

Well, screw him. She didn't owe him, or any of them, anything. Turning her back to him, Jane walked across the room, head forward, not meeting anyone's gaze.

Damn Devon for putting her in this position. She did not like garnering attention to herself, and she certainly wasn't comfortable with confrontation, although she was learning at a rapid pace how to take care of herself.

Where was he anyway?

Jane stopped in a quiet corner of the room and dared a glance around. She was partially hidden by a large potted plant and prayed that somehow she could just blend into the surroundings.

"Tough crowd tonight, huh?"

Jane's spirits sank as she heard yet another masculine voice from just behind her. Would this evening never end?

She nodded, but didn't smile. No sense encouraging anyone.

"Matt Wilkens."

From her peripheral vision, she saw a hand being extended in her direction. Basic politeness forced her to accept the handshake, but she didn't offer her name in return.

"I haven't seen you before," he commented.

Jane nearly groaned aloud. Was she going to hear every line in the book this evening? She started planning her escape. Maybe she could somehow hail a cab home, although Devon hadn't let her bring a handbag, and she doubted any cab driver would give her a free ride, no matter what kind of outfit she wore.

Before she could respond, the man laughed. "That totally sounded like a pickup line, didn't it?"

She laughed sarcastically, "Yeah, it did." She was tired of playing games and even more tired of being polite.

"I'm sorry." He seemed sincere. His deep, articulate voice made her turn her head in his direction. Matt Wilkens was an older, gray-haired man, perfectly distinguished in a well-tailored suit. The expression on his face was curious, but not leering. He smiled at her. "It's just that I know most everyone here, so I was surprised to see a face I didn't recognize."

Jane wasn't sure how to respond. Friendly or not, she didn't know the man standing beside her and, furthermore, had no idea why he would even need to know who she was.

What had he said his name was again? Matt Wilson? No. Matt Wilkens. Yes, that was it.

Suddenly, a light bulb went off in her head. She turned her head back towards the entrance of the venue. As she thought, Wilkens was one of the names on the banner on the wall. Jane felt a knot begin to form in the pit of her stomach. This man must be a partner in the firm hosting the party.

Jane blushed again, somehow even more embarrassed to be caught in her current presentation in front of this sophisticated man.

Feeling positively mortified, Jane apologized, "I'm sorry for being so rude. I'm just a little out of sorts tonight. My name is Jane Rawlings."

She offered her hand again and he took it in a firm handshake. "Nice to meet you, Ms. Rawlings."

His greeting was polite, but his expression was still inquisitive. He was obviously wondering what she was doing there.

She swallowed. "I'm here with my husband, Devon Rawlings."

She prayed Devon's name would trigger a response from the partner, but he still had a polite, but curious smile pasted on his face.

Luckily, at that moment, Devon reappeared, snatching the drink from her hand. "There you are. Took you long enough."

He started to walk away, but Jane pulled at his coat sleeve. "Devon, this is Matt Wilkens."

Again, she hoped for some sort of recognition and some explanation of what they were doing here.

Matt held out his hand and smiled pleasantly. "Nice

to meet you, Mr. Rawlings. Forgive me for monopolizing your wife."

Devon did not take the man's hand and instead said with a sneer as he walked away, drink in hand, "Forget it. You can have her."

Time stood still as the words floated like daggers in the air. Jane felt the blood rush from her face and then surge back as humiliation seared through her. Tears sprang to her eyes, and she looked at the nice man standing beside her with huge, sad eyes. "I'm sorry. I don't know what got into him. He's not usually like that." But even she didn't hear any conviction in her voice.

Matt smiled understandingly. There was something almost paternal in his expression. She could tell he felt sorry for her. She didn't want sympathy; but, at the same time, she was grateful it was sympathy and not amusement. Or acceptance.

"Can I get you anything?" Matt asked kindly.

"How about a jacket and a ride home?" she answered honestly. She was tired of playing games.

Matt immediately started to shrug out of his tuxedo coat. Jane reluctantly smiled and placed her hand on his arm. "I was being sarcastic."

He stopped, but replied, "I was being serious."

Jane nodded and said sadly, "My husband wouldn't like it."

Matt nodded in understanding. "I imagine not."

Jane closed her mouth. That simple statement was more than she had revealed to anyone in years. But she felt raw and exposed. And betrayed. If she stayed much longer, she was afraid of what else she might say to this understanding man, who was just a kind stranger. She had too much at stake to risk offering too much information. Instead, she said with a smile that didn't reach her eyes, "Thank you for the offer, though."

She walked away when Matt Wilkens touched her arm lightly. She turned to look back at him. He said, "My offer was sincere. If I can help you in any way, please let me know."

Jane nodded silently. She was afraid that if she spoke, she might break down completely.

Making her way through the crowded room, Jane looked for Devon. Part of her didn't want to find him, especially in his current nasty mood, but she hoped that maybe he had had enough fun at her expense and would be willing to leave the party. Or at least let her go. At this point, she no longer cared what he was doing here – she just wanted out.

When, after thirty minutes, she still hadn't located him, Jane's patience wore out.

She was tired of the charade.

In fact, she was tired, in general.

She had spent all of her life learning to control her emotions, like a puppet. Her life so far had been nothing but an act–she had spent her years playing a part–the only part she ever knew. Jane had once thought she had everything she wanted, but she knew she had never had real feelings for Devon–or maybe for anyone. She had become so numb emotionally, she wasn't sure she even knew what true feelings were. She had been taught to be soft and compliant on the outside–but on the inside she was strong. Stronger than she ever imagined she could be. Stronger than anyone, especially Devon, would ever realize.

She was ready to look out for herself. All she needed

was a sign. She didn't know when it would happen. But, when it did she would be ready.

She spotted Matt Wilkens across the room. Without allowing herself to ponder what proper manners would entail, she made her way to him.

"I'd like to take you up on your offer," she said, without preamble.

Matt excused himself from the group he stood near and escorted her to a more private area.

"My coat or a ride home?" he asked with an understanding smile.

"A ride home, please." Jane hoped she wasn't going to have to explain herself further. Her situation was both mortifying and depressing.

She didn't have to worry. Matt took her arm gently and led her to the front entrance where a valet attendant jumped to attention. "How can I help you, Mr. Wilkens?"

Matt smiled at the man. "If you could have one of the drivers take Ms. Rawlings home, I would appreciate it."

"Certainly, sir." The attendant moved to his station and picked up the radio.

"I don't want to put you in any trouble," Jane said sincerely.

"It's no trouble at all," Matt assured her.

Moments later a sleek black Town Car pulled into the circular drive. Matt leaned in and spoke briefly to the driver and then helped Jane into the back seat.

"It was a pleasure to meet you," he said and then lowered his voice. "I hope things work out for you."

"They will," Jane responded firmly.

She would make sure of it.

****

"Congratulations, attorney of the year," Brad whispered in her ear.

Stephanie grinned and looked at the plaque in her hands. It was a silly award, but she felt proud anyway. Everyone in the firm worked as hard as she did – she had just been lucky enough to close the biggest deal.

When she felt Brad's lips move from her ear to her neck, she swatted him away. "Stop that. Someone could see us."

Actually, the couple had moved outside to the atrium for privacy, but there were partygoers moving in and out frequently enough that Stephanie felt uncomfortable showing any obvious affection. Although she absolutely wanted to. It was still too soon.

"I don't care if anyone sees us," Brad complained, but he straightened up and stood next to her – very close. It was as much as he was willing to give.

She smiled and leaned her head into him. "I know."

"Seriously, when am I going to get to let everyone know that we are a couple?" he asked with a smile.

It was the first time he had made such a statement. On one hand, she loved that he thought of them as a couple. On the other hand, it left a pit in the center of her gut because it meant she had to confront Devon once and for all. Brad didn't deserve that kind of treatment.

Brad could feel the tension in her shoulders and immediately backed off. "Do I at least get to take you home and celebrate properly?"

"Of course," she responded immediately. Even though the prospect petrified her, Stephanie knew she didn't want to spend the night alone. She wanted to be with Brad.

"Can I get you a drink?" Brad asked, accepting the

situation.

Stephanie thought for a moment. The night was still young, and she had the knowledge of a whole night with Brad to look forward to. "Sure. I did just win attorney of the year." Then she held out the plaque in her hands. "Would you mind taking this to the car when you go in? I feel silly carrying it around."

"Really?" Brad frowned. "Because if I had won that award, I would have it hanging around my neck like a medal."

Stephanie laughed. "You would not. Anyway, it's not like it means anything."

Brad looked at her. "I bet Wilkens would disagree."

"Well, yeah, Matt is happy because that contract brought in a ton of money for the firm. If he really wanted to show his gratitude, he'd give me a big fat raise." She spoke in a playful voice, clearly joking. She was well compensated for her efforts and had no complaints.

Brad shook his head in mock wonder. "That's my girl. Modest as always."

He took the plaque and planted a kiss on her lips. "I'll be back before you can even miss me."

Stephanie smiled and said, "Too late."

He winked at her and disappeared inside the venue.

Stephanie turned around to admire the beautiful landscaping on the terrace. She didn't want to go inside and socialize with her colleagues. She had too much on her mind. She just wanted to wait quietly for Brad to return. With him next to her, she felt complete. It was a beautiful evening – the wind was blowing softly in the warm air. She was glad she didn't have on a jacket. The warm breeze felt great against her bare shoulders. If she could just bottle this exact moment and savor it – it was perfect. A gorgeous evening. A beautiful dress. The company of a man she was free to fall in love with. She didn't want the moment to end.

"Hey you."

Stephanie stiffened as the hairs on her neck stood at attention. As if moving in slow motion, she turned around. Devon smiled at her and held out a glass of wine. "Fancy meeting you here."

Stephanie shook her head and took a step backward. "I don't…" She glanced quickly about, looking for Brad, but he was nowhere to be seen. For that, she was grateful. She frowned at Devon. "What are you doing here?"

"I came to see you," Devon smiled at her, but there was a dangerous gleam in his eye. One she had never seen before. He placed the wine glass in her hand, saying, "Aren't you glad to see me?"

There were several words that could describe Stephanie's feelings – glad was not one of them. She was at a private business function. What was Devon doing? She set the glass on the railing behind her and asked, "How did you know I would be here?" She purposely hadn't mentioned the event.

Devon reached into his coat pocket and pulled out a dirty, food-stained invitation and held it up.

Stephanie's mouth dropped open. Her memory flashed back to the day she had found the lid off her garbage can. Incredulously, she asked, "You dug through my trash?"

Devon shrugged. "I know. I certainly never imagined that I would have to find out things that way. But, since you've been lying and hiding things from me – I really had no choice."

The sinister tone of his voice sent a chill down her spine. She realized he had her cornered on the terrace where she was not clearly visible. She made a move to step around him, saying dismissively, "This is a business function. I had to attend. It's no big deal."

Devon took a step sideways, blocking her. "Oh, but it is a big deal."

Stephanie pinched her lips together. She knew she was trapped. If she made another move, Devon was going to cause a scene in front of her colleagues. She didn't want that. With resignation, she asked, "What do you want, Devon?"

"I want to be with you," he replied.

It was a ridiculous statement. He was trying to goad her. She couldn't tell if he was drunk or crazy, but the fact that he had dug through her trash and shown up at a private business function was so out of character that Stephanie was afraid of what he might do next. And she was even more afraid of what might happen if Brad came back. She would never, ever, be willing to compromise Brad. Devon was her problem. And she needed to take care of it. But first, she needed to get Devon out of this environment. "This is probably not a good time...."

Devon cut her off. "It's the perfect time. See - I've brought my wife. I'm ready to go inside and introduce you to her. I'll tell her everything."

"What?" Stephanie's mouth hung open, flabbergasted by his audacity. She couldn't process his words. "What are you talking about?"

"Isn't that what you wanted? For me to pronounce my love for you in front of everyone?"

"No," Stephanie protested vehemently. "That is not what I want."

"Sure it is," Devon countered. He grabbed her forearm. Hard. "So, let's go inside. Let's do this."

Stephanie yanked her arm away. Her skin twisted and burned beneath the strength of his grip, but she got it loose. "Are you crazy?"

Devon moved his face very close to hers. "Yes, I am."

Stephanie stepped backward, tripping over her dress and nearly stumbling. She looked around as if to make a run for it, but Devon blocked her exit. He lowered his voice, but his eyes remained dark and foreboding. "I'm crazy about you. I want to be with you." He dropped his tone to a menacing level. "Forever."

Truly afraid for her safety, Stephanie fought to maintain a semblance of calm. "What about your wife? She needs you."

Devon shook his head vehemently. "My wife is not who I thought she was. She's inside right now whoring herself out to every man who will look at her."

From what she knew, Stephanie doubted that was even remotely true. Clearly, Devon had lost touch with reality.

He pulled her to him, speaking rapidly. "You can replace her." He stroked her cheek, and she flinched, but he didn't notice. He spoke in a dreamy voice, more to himself than to her directly. "You can be everything she isn't."

He sounded desperate. And delusional.

"Devon..." Stephanie searched for the words to get through to him. She felt like an actress playing the lead role in a bad movie. In those movies; however, things didn't always end well for the heroine. "Let's not do this here." She didn't know what she would do if Devon made a scene in front of her colleagues. More importantly, she didn't know what would happen if Brad returned.

Grabbing her hand, Devon forced her across the patio towards the ballroom. "No, this is the perfect place. I want my wife to see what happens to anyone who betrays me."

He stopped and stared into her eyes. "I know you won't betray me. Because if you did – I would kill you, too."

Stephanie yanked on her hand, but Devon had an ironclad grip on her wrist. Even as she stumbled, he hauled her to her feet as they stood in front of the glass window looking into the ballroom. His breaths wheezed as he labored, and his cheeks flushed a bright red. "It's time to show everyone who is in control."

"Devon..." Stephanie frantically worked to free herself from his grip.

Suddenly, Devon dropped her hand and placed his palm on the window. "That bitch," he screamed, pushing Stephanie aside as he tore open the glass door to the ballroom, tearing inside.

Stephanie didn't stop to see what he was talking about. She turned and ran across the patio, climbing over the brick wall surrounding the terrace. The skirt of her long dress snagged on the rock wall, and Stephanie ripped the delicate fabric loose. She didn't care if the dress was ruined. She knew she would never wear it again. Blindly, she ran down the sidewalk towards the car, afraid to look behind her in case Devon saw her.

A block away, she spotted Brad. He smiled and waved when he saw her and then stopped abruptly as he processed her disheveled appearance. "What's going on?"

She grabbed his hand and pulled him with her. "We have to go. We have to get out of here, right now."

"Stephanie," Brad tried to make her slow down, but she shook her head and pulled away.

"There's no time."

Stephanie kept running and Brad spun around and took after her. At the car, she jumped into the passenger seat and waved her hand vehemently as Brad stood at the open door. "Get in and drive."

But Brad held his ground. He placed his hands on the roof of the car. "Not until you tell me what is going on."

"I promise," she said rapidly, touching his cheek. "I will tell you everything, but you have to get in and get us out of here. Right now." She knew she was putting him in a dangerous situation. More dangerous than he could possibly imagine. But she had no choice.

Latching on to the panic in her voice, Brad rounded the front of the car and slid into the driver's seat. As he pulled out onto the road and away from the venue, Stephanie kept her eyes glued to the rearview mirror. The street behind them was empty.

"Where are we going?" he asked, keeping his eyes on the road.

"I'm not sure," Stephanie admitted. She was out of her league. And she was afraid. "I don't know what to do."

"Why don't you start at the beginning?" he suggested.

And, because she had fallen in love with Brad, she did.

****

"Get your hands off my wife," Devon shouted, pushing aside the valet attendant and standing nose-to-nose with Matt Wilkens.

"Devon," Jane admonished, horrified.

Devon did not acknowledge her. Instead, he glared at the man before him. "What do you think you are doing?"

Keeping his composure, Matt said simply, "Offering your wife a ride home since you obviously don't have the good manners to do so yourself."

Devon puffed out his chest and raised his fists to chest level, looking as if he were about to punch the older man. As if by magic, a set of large security guards appeared on either side of Matt. Devon eyed the two men and lowered his fists, but his expression remained thunderous. "I decide if and when my wife leaves."

Matt smiled. "Seems to me she's perfectly capable of making that decision on her own."

"Back off," Devon hissed. "This is none of your concern."

"My guests' needs are always my concern," Matt contradicted.

"She is not your guest."

"Actually," Matt said, "Ms. Rawlings has been a perfectly charming guest and is welcome at my event any time. You; however," Matt gave Devon a steely look and said firmly, "are not."

"Fine," Devon spat and turned back to his wife. "Come on. Let's go."

But Jane shook her head. "No."

Devon's jaw literally fell open. "What did you say to me?"

"I said no." Jane's voice was strong and clear. "I'm

not going with you. Not now. Not ever."

Devon reached out as if to grab her by the arm. Both Matt and his security guards moved to intervene, but Jane raised a hand, holding them in place. She turned her gaze to her husband. Her voice was firm and clear and there was a hint of steel in her expression. She was not afraid. "I'm going to take Matt up on his generous offer to have his driver take me home. I suggest you gather your coat and leave as well."

Devon's face grew red. He clearly didn't like being told what to do. Especially, not by Jane. If they had been alone, she knew he would have attacked her physically. Even now, she could see the conflict on his face as he struggled with whether or not to cause a scene in public. He glanced over his shoulder to see Matt and security still watching the conversation intently. He turned back to Jane. "Fine. Go home. I have some things to take care of, anyway." He pointed his finger at her. "But we are not done here. We *will* continue this conversation when I get home." From his emphasis on the word will, she knew he would be planning something particularly brutal.

He couldn't scare her anymore.

Jane smiled grimly, shook her head, and took a step towards the car. "I won't be home when you get there."

With Matt's security guards so close, Devon didn't approach her again, but he said in a dangerous tone, "You are making a huge mistake. If you leave now, I will make sure you regret your decision for the rest of your life."

Jane smiled sadly. "I have too many decisions I regret already. I don't think one more will hurt me."

"I won't let you leave," Devon said savagely. "You

belong to me. I will take away everything that is important to you."

Jane met his stare. "You already have."

As she slid into the back seat of the Town Car, Devon took a step toward the car and immediately one of Matt's security guards moved forward and took his arm.

She heard Matt's voice as he said, "I think it's time for you to leave. These men will help you get your things."

Devon yanked his arm from the guard's grip. He spun around and stood nose-to-nose with Matt. "I don't need your help."

Then he turned back to Jane and snarled, "Bitch."

As Matt's security guard lunged for him again, Devon fled back inside the venue.

Matt told one of his men, "Keep an eye on him. Make sure he leaves."

The man nodded and took off in the direction Devon was headed.

Matt turned to Jane, who sat ramrod stiff in the backseat of the Town Car. He went to the car, placed his hand on the hood, and leaned in slightly, keeping his voice soft. "Are you okay?"

Jane nodded and smiled at Matt. "Thank you for your help. I'm sorry you had to see that."

"I'm worried about you," he said honestly. "Do you want me to send one of my men along with you? To make sure you're okay."

But Jane shook her head. "I appreciate the offer, but this is not your fight."

Matt straightened, and took a moment to think, as if he were trying to formulate his words. Finally, he said,

"I know he is your husband, but he does seem a little unstable." He paused and then added, "And possibly dangerous. I can have the authorities meet you at your house–just in case."

"No," Jane said quickly, but softly. "I meant what I said. I won't be home when he gets there."

Matt still looked unconvinced. "If you're sure…"

"I am," she said with conviction and after another moment, Matt nodded, but added sincerely, "You have my card. If you need anything…"

"You have been very kind," Jane cut him off softly, but added in a firm voice, "I know what I need to do."

"Okay then," Matt hesitated for a moment and then lowered his voice. "In spite of the circumstances, it has been a pleasure meeting you."

Jane smiled in return, and Matt tapped on the hood of the car, signaling his driver to exit. As the sleek Town Car pulled away from the curb, Jane dropped her head, allowing a single tear to roll down her cheek. Despite the bravado she'd shown in front of Matt, Devon still frightened her; but she knew this time, she had no choice. She had to defend herself.

Otherwise, she was certain she would end up dead.

****

Devon crashed through the crowded event, pushing aside anyone standing in his path, until he reached the back doors.

"Stephanie," he called out, pushing open the heavy doors, "forget about my wife. That bitch is gone. We can be together just like we planned. Let's get out of here."

He skidded to a halt in the empty terrace. He spun around wildly, calling, "Stephanie – where are you?"

Matt's security guard slammed through the glass

doors onto the terrace. When he saw Devon alone outside, he stopped at the entrance, watching silently.

Devon seemed not to notice him.

With a look of disgust, Devon paced the small area, mumbling to himself, "Where did she go? I told her to wait here…"

After several minutes of pacing the area, he suddenly stopped and stared at the brick wall separating the terrace from the sidewalk beyond. Clenching his fists, he walked to the fence. He dropped to one knee and picked up an object from the ground. He examined it closely for a long moment and then stood up, screaming in rage.

"That BITCH."

Just as the security guard took a step forward to subdue him, Devon jumped over the fence and took off down the street. The guard went to the wall leaning over to look down the street, but Devon had already disappeared around the corner. With a shake of his head, he started to walk away. A shot of color caught his peripheral vision, and he stopped and leaned down to examine further.

A scrap of royal blue fabric was caught in the branches of the small hedge near the fence.

Chapter Fifteen

"What all do you need out of the bathroom?" Brad's
voice sounded calm, but Stephanie was well aware of the
mounting tension in the room.

On the way home, she had filled him in with the
details of her relationship with Devon and his increasing
paranoia around her ending with the events that had just
occurred at the party.

Brad's initial response was to call the police and let
them handle it, but Stephanie had balked at going to that
extreme. In spite of recent events, she couldn't just see
what calling the police would accomplish. Devon had
been acting delusional and had, in fact, threatened her;
but he hadn't physically harmed her, and in her heart, she
didn't want to believe he was capable of true violence.
Brad had disagreed, but settled for insisting she leave her
apartment immediately and go with him to his house at
least for the evening.

Stephanie had agreed without much protest. Truth
be told, even though she didn't think Devon would hurt
her, her nerves were shot, and she knew she would feel
more secure somewhere else for the evening. She was
thankful Brad had offered her a place to stay. After
everything she had revealed, she wasn't sure he would
even speak to her again.

The royal blue gown laying on the floor glared at her
as she moved about her room. She was fresh from a hot

215

shower and had donned her favorite sweats and a T-shirt. Her face was void of makeup, but she didn't have the energy to attempt any makeup. Seeing the dress brought a fresh fit of emotion to her. It was just like Devon to come in and ruin what was supposed to be her evening. Even when he didn't know she had something special happening, he managed to upstage her. She had put her life on hold for someone who absolutely had no respect for her.

"Argh..." Humiliated, she grabbed the torn evening gown and shoved it into the back of her closet. She never, ever, wanted to see that dress again.

"Everything okay?" Brad called from the bathroom.

"Yes," she said, more quietly, taking a seat on the bed. The hot shower and change of clothes had helped her feel better, at least physically. She would need some time to recover emotionally, though. She hadn't realized how much daily strain she carried with her until she had unloaded her situation this evening. She had never told another soul about her relationship with Devon. Not family, not friends, not even a journal. It had been her own private heaven...and hell. Even though she had left out some of the more humiliating aspects, the story wasn't pretty. She now fully realized how terrible she came across–she was the mistress of a married man. Nothing but a glamorized prostitute, if you boiled it down.

Brad had listened to every word she said without comment. When she was done, he led her into the bathroom and turned on the shower for her. As she showered and cried, he had found her suitcase and left it open on the bed. He had gathered her things without speaking. His expression was neutral, and Stephanie had no idea of what he might be thinking.

She wouldn't be surprised if Brad decided he didn't want to have anything to do with her once this immediate crisis was over. He was too much of a gentleman to allow her to face a potentially dangerous situation alone; but, once that was over, she couldn't blame him if he bolted.

"Which one is yours?" Brad asked, standing in the bathroom's doorway holding up a yellow toothbrush and a green one. Stephanie swallowed the lump in her throat as she realized the extra toothbrush belonged to Devon. "The yellow one," she mumbled, feeling shame crawl through her veins. The events of the evening overwhelmed her again, and a new batch of tears started falling. She wasn't much of a crier by nature, but recent events had left her feeling emotional and raw.

Brad tossed the toothbrush into her overnight bag and crossed over to the bed, putting his arms around her shoulders. "It's okay," he soothed. "Everything is going to be okay."

Stephanie shook her head. "I've made such a mess of things." She dropped her head into her hands and mumbled through her sobs. "And now I don't know what to do."

Brad hugged her closer. "You have to talk to him. You have to tell him he can't be a part of your life anymore."

Stephanie nodded and wiped her eyes. "I know. I've been meaning to, but a part of me has been afraid. It's been easier to just avoid him." She raised her eyes to him. "And now I've put both of us in this awful situation. Can you ever forgive me?"

She expected to see a flicker of disappointment cross his features, but instead, he smiled. "There is nothing to forgive. You are going to get through this. I am going to help you."

She shrugged out of his embrace. "How can you be so nice to me? After everything I just told you?"

Brad's answer was simple. "I'm in love with you."

"How can you say that?" she countered. Hearing her own voice tell the story out loud, she didn't even love herself. No matter how many times over the years, she had tried to validate it, the bottom line remained that she was having an affair with a married man. She didn't deserve to be loved.

Brad reached for her chin and turned her to face him. He held her eyes with his warm brown ones. "You didn't do anything wrong…"

When she opened her mouth to protest, he backtracked. "Okay, maybe you made some questionable decisions…"

When she raised an eyebrow and held out her hand to stop him, he grabbed her hand and held it to his chest. "But your intentions were good. You were in love."

She shook her head vehemently.

He nodded. "It's okay. Maybe love isn't the right word. Still, you were under the spell of a ruthless, controlling person. He's the one who is at fault. He manipulated the situation. He manipulated you."

Stephanie blinked back the tears. She knew in her heart what Brad said was true. She had let herself be manipulated. And it was so much worse than even Brad knew. She hadn't even told him about the ten o'clock calls. She didn't think she ever would be able to. Now that her eyes were wide open, it was easy to see how destructive the relationship had been.

A fresh set of tears started up. "I don't deserve you,"

she cried.

Brad smiled softly, "I'm sorry you feel that way– because you are stuck with me." His tone hardened. "I'm not going to let anyone hurt you."

He stood up. "Now, finish your packing. We need to get out of here."

Stephanie nodded and went to her dresser drawer, pulling out shorts and undergarments and throwing them into her open travel bag. She didn't know how long she would be gone, but she wanted to make sure she had enough to last her. She had already called the office and let her assistant know she would be taking a couple of days of vacation. Her plan was to disappear from any place Devon might come looking for her. She would set up a meeting with him in a neutral public place and tell him in no uncertain terms that they were done.

The thought of confronting Devon suddenly brought an image of his wife to her mind. She didn't know the woman, but couldn't help but think of Devon's rage when he looked through the glass at the reception. She was thankful it had given her the opportunity to escape Devon's delusional rantings but wondered if his wife had taken the brunt of his anger.

Stephanie turned her head to look at Brad, who was folding the clothes she had thrown into her suitcase and placing them in neater stacks. A rush of gratitude washed over her. No matter what happened, she knew Brad would be there for her to take care of her and protect her.

Devon's wife might not have such good fortune.

"I'll be right back." She walked into the living room.

She knew it wasn't her place, but she felt like she owed the woman something. She had taken so much, and she wanted to somehow help if she could.

Reaching for her phone, she searched her contact list and texted the simple message. BE SAFE.

She issued a silent prayer that Devon's wife was alone when the text came through. She certainly didn't want to cause any additional harm. She just wanted things to be over.

As she was about to walk back into the bedroom, her phone buzzed. Heart pounding, she picked it up.

I'M SAFE AT HOME. YOU TAKE CARE OF YOU.

The tone was ominous, and Stephanie felt a shiver of fear run down her spine. Until this moment, she hadn't truly been afraid of Devon – she had just wanted to move on with her own life. She had figured that Devon ran after his wife and the two of them had gone home. With any luck, Devon would sleep off whatever he was on and tomorrow would be a new day. What if her predication had been off?

As if reading her mind, a pair of headlights streamed into the alleyway.

Brad immediately came into the living room. "Who is that?"

Stephanie shook her head, but she knew. By the pounding in her chest and the weakness in her knees. She knew.

They stood side by side as a car screeched into the driveway, pulling in behind her parked car. Stephanie felt a rush of relief that Brad had chosen to park in the visitor lot of her complex.

"I take it that's not the pizza delivery guy." Brad's attempt at humor fell flat as neither one of them attempted to smile.

Stephanie sighed heavily and turned from the

window. "It's him," she said, anxious, yet relieved a little at the same time. She didn't want to put things off any longer. She wanted to end things right now and move on with her life. It was way overdue. Devon might threaten and cajole, but, really what was he going to do? He had a wife to go home to. He didn't need her.

"I'm calling the police," Brad said, reaching for his phone.

Stephanie placed her hand over his. "Not yet. Let me talk to him. It's time. Let's just end it."

"I'm not leaving you alone with him," Brad protested sternly.

Stephanie didn't blame him, but having Brad present wasn't going to help the situation. This was her mess, and she needed to fix it herself.

She placed her hand on Brad's arm. She knew she didn't have much time. "I need you to wait in the bedroom." She adopted her best attorney voice. "I will be fine. He's not going to hurt me."

"I don't think…" Brad was clearly not done.

Stephanie heard footsteps on the stairs. She gave Brad a push towards the bedroom. "There's no time. Please, I know what I'm doing."

Against Brad's protests, she maneuvered him into the bedroom. She had barely shut the door when the knob on the front door turned. When the lock clicked in place, there was a hesitation followed by rapid pounding on the door. "Stephanie, it's me. Let me in." Devon was used to having the front door unlocked when he arrived. Stephanie was expected to be ready and waiting for him at all times.

His voice didn't sound as manic as before, but Stephanie made sure she turned the lock and stepped quickly away from the door in case he made any sudden move to grab her.

Devon practically ran into the room as soon as the door unlocked. "Stephanie," he said, taking in rapid breaths as if he had run from the car. His tuxedo looked wrinkled, and his hair flopped wildly across his forehead. For a man who took great pride in his appearance, his disheveled look threw Stephanie off a little. He crossed the room and placed his hands on her forearms, not quite hugging her. "Thank God I found you."

Stephanie ignored his comment. "What are you doing here, Devon?"

Devon straightened up and looked at her. His expression was confused as he explained like it were the most obvious thing in the world, "I came to see you. When you disappeared from the party, I got worried."

"I didn't disappear from the party, Devon," she replied. "I left. And came home."

"But why?" Devon continued to play innocent. "I thought we were going to leave together."

Stephanie was incredulous. Did he really think she would buy this act after the way he behaved earlier?

"No, Devon," she said firmly. "We were never going to leave together. You came to a business event and harassed me. That was not okay with me."

Devon reached for her again, but Stephanie took a step backward out of his grip. "I'm sorry, baby. I didn't mean to upset you. I just wanted to be with you. I love you." He lowered his voice to the deep seductive tone Stephanie had once found so sexy. Now she realized how manipulative and condescending it really was.

She took a deep breath and closed her eyes, imagining Brad in the other room, listening. She had to be strong for him. He deserved so much more. Devon must have read something in her expression as she thought about Brad because his tone sharpened as he asked pointedly, "You love me, too, don't you?"

Afraid her pounding heart would burst through her chest, Stephanie stated, "I don't want to do this anymore."

Devon stopped and stared at her. His eyes narrowed. "Do what?"

Meeting his gaze, she elaborated, "Sneak around like this. Lie to my friends about what I'm doing. Lie to my family. What we had," she used the past tense intentionally, "was never a real relationship. You are married."

She was upset to find herself close to tears. She had said these same things to him so many times before, but this time, at this moment, she knew it was the last time she was going to say them. Because, this time, at this moment, she knew the truth. With a note of finality in her voice, she said, "I deserve better. I deserve a husband who loves me. And a family…" The thought of Brad waiting for her in the bedroom brought tears to her eyes again. She wanted all of those things – with Brad. She hoped it wasn't too late.

Devon mistook her emotion and immediately made an effort to placate her. He dropped to one knee and took her hand in his, saying passionately. "Baby, I know how you feel. And I'm ready to give all of that to you. I am."

But…

Devon always said everything she wanted to hear and then paused with the appropriate woe-be-gone expression with the word *but* hovering on his lips. If she didn't stop him, he would have to say something like,

"But, my wife needs me…or I just need a little more time…" or one of the other ready-to-go excuses. There were too many to remember, and they all started to run together. The pause beforehand was so Stephanie could rush to his side and take Devon into her arms, so he didn't have to say anything further.

Stephanie, however, was done. She removed her hand from his and took a step away, turning her back to him. "You need to leave, now, Devon. You need to go home to your wife."

Misunderstanding her meaning, Devon continued on with his normal pitch. He stood up and said, "I'm going to talk to Jane. Tonight. I promise." He took a step in her direction. "I just need to let her down easily. She so fragile…"

"Stop." Stephanie turned back to Devon and held up a hand. As much as she just wanted him out of her house, she couldn't hold her tongue any longer. "Just stop," she repeated with disgust. "We both know that it's not Jane," she said, revulsion creeping into her tone. "It was never Jane. It was the money. It was always the money, wasn't it?"

Devon stopped short, any trace of passion fleeing from his expression. He glared at her, eyes dark, and said brusquely, "What exactly are you implying?"

"I'm not implying anything," Stephanie countered. "I'm straight up saying – you'll never leave your wife because you don't want to give up the money. The money belongs to her. She has all the leverage, not you."

Devon's face turned an ugly shade of purple, and a vein popped out in his forehead. "How do you know about that?"

Stephanie realized too late that she had revealed too

much. How would she know that unless she had been in contact with Devon's wife?

With a sinking feeling in her stomach, she tried to backtrack. She said, "It doesn't matter." Devon took a step toward her, and she took another step backward, feeling the wall press up against her back. Devon had her pinned against the wall, and she felt a trace of fear slide up her spine. Still, she forced her voice to remain firm and calm. She knew Brad was listening. She was thankful that he couldn't see her precarious situation. She prayed that as long as she kept her voice steady, he would remain hidden, out of harm's way. "It's over Devon. I don't want to see you anymore."

"It's over when I say it's over." Devon reached for her, and she slid past him and ran across the room. As Devon began tossing papers and pillows from her sofa and end table, Stephanie stopped at the entrance to her bedroom.

As she feared, the knob to her bedroom door turned, and Stephanie frantically pulled it shut again. She would not put Brad in harm's way. She stood in front of the door as Brad hissed from inside. "Let go. I'm coming out there."

"Not yet," she called, speaking from the corner of her mouth, hoping Devon didn't notice. "I'm okay."

Luckily, Devon was too preoccupied to hear. He spotted her phone lying on the coffee table and pounced on it.

Stephanie's heart dropped.

With a smirk in her direction, he pressed the send button on her phone, pulling up the last message. The one from his wife.

She closed her eyes as he scrolled through the text

history, knowing the information that it contained.

"You lying bitch."

Stephanie didn't know if he was talking about her or his wife, but she knew she wasn't going to be able to hold Brad back any longer.

As her bedroom door opened, Devon stormed past her, not seeing her or anything around her. As he stood through the front door, he turned one last time. Stephanie pulled the door shut once more, hiding Brad just in time.

Devon's voice was deadly. "I'll be back."

"No," Stephanie held her ground. "Don't come back, Devon. I won't be here." She knew now that she would never return to this place. Maybe she would start a new life with Brad, or maybe she would end up on her own. Either way, the nightmare that had been her life for the past three years would be over.

Or would it?

Devon didn't move toward her, but she could see the rage in his eyes as he repeated, "You're going to leave me?" A look of disgust filled his face. "You're no better than she is. Fine, then, leave if you want. I will be back. I will find you."

He slammed the door shut and a moment later she heard the squeal of tires as he tore out of the driveway down the street. Stephanie released her grip on the bedroom door and collapsed into Brad's arm as he opened it.

He held her tightly, and she was grateful for his strength. She felt as if she had run a marathon. They both heard the squeal of tires as Devon's car sped through the alley.

"I'm calling the police," Brad reached for her phone. "That lunatic has to be stopped."

He was right. Devon was dangerous. With a thankful smile, Stephanie nodded and took the phone from his hand. "I'll take care of it."

"Are you sure?"

Stephanie nodded again. "Can you take my bags to the car?" She held up her phone, indicating that she was going to make a call. "I'll meet you down there."

Brad hesitated, but then went into the bedroom without further comments and grabbed her bags. He kissed her softly on the lips and said, "I'll wait for you in the car."

With tears in her eyes, she smiled at him. She was lucky. She had Brad to help her pick up the pieces. One way or another, she knew she was going to be okay. Devon's wife might not have the same luck.

Stephanie picked up her phone and typed in an all too familiar number.

GET OUT OF THE HOUSE. HE'S GOING TO HURT YOU.

Chapter Sixteen

Jane barely responded as her phone buzzed beside her. She had been half expecting it. Even though Devon had told her he would be home for her, she knew he would visit his mistress first. Once her eyes had opened, his patterns were actually very predictable.

Although she had told him she wouldn't be home when he arrived, that was a lie as well.

She was inside her closet - folding clothes. Her closet was so full no one would ever suspect that a large portion of her wardrobe, excluding the silk nightgowns and cashmere sweaters, had been shipped to an undisclosed location in another state. Her room, her house, her life was in perfect order – just as it always was. Not a thing was out of place.

She slipped a folded sweater into its place on the shelf and glanced over at the phone sitting atop her dressing table next to her oversized Louis Vuitton handbag. Never again would she have to hide any of her personal belongings. She was done being afraid.

The screen glowed a gray-blue, and Jane took a deep breath and left the closet. It was time. She picked up the phone and read the words.

HE'S GOING TO HURT YOU.

The ominous words actually brought a smile to Jane's lips. No, Devon was never going to hurt her again.

When she didn't respond, her phone lit up again.

I'M CALLING THE POLICE.

This time, Jane typed quickly on her keypad.

THAT WON'T BE NECESSARY.

She would call the police herself. When the time was right.

Ten minutes later, Jane sat calmly on the bed, hands folded on her lap, when the front door slammed open. She could hear Devon crash through the living room. Something glass hit the floor–probably a vase. Jane remained seated.

"Jane, get down here."

Devon's voice shook with rage. She didn't need a visual to imagine the veins popping in his forehead or the darkness shining in his eyes. Jane still didn't respond, but she placed her hand on the oversized Louis Vuitton tote bag beside her on the bed. Her heart beat at an erratic pace. She knew what she had to do, but she was afraid. It would take every ounce of courage she possessed, but she would stand up for herself. Not just for her sake, but for everything her mother had sacrificed before her.

"Did you not hear me?" Devon shouted as he stormed up the stairs and into their room. He stood in the doorway, panting from the effort of running up the stairs.

"No, I heard you," Jane replied calmly, looking him in the eye.

Devon strode across the room and stood in front of her, glaring down at her, fury in his eyes. "How dare you?" He screamed, spittle bursting from his lips. "How dare you talk to Stephanie behind my back?"

Jane did not flinch or try to get up, but continued clutching her bag tightly. "You mean your mistress?" she asked directly. Gone was the mild, timid voice that Devon was accustomed to. Jane's voice was strong and firm, betraying none of the anxiety she felt inside.

Devon took a literal step backward at her abrupt response. His eyes were still black, but his facial expression went from rage to confusion. He clearly didn't know how to react to losing the upper hand. "She's not my mistress," he stumbled over his words, trying to backtrack.

"Of course she is." Jane cut him off. "Let's not lie. There have been too many lies already."

"I'm not lying…" he started, working to regain his composure. He ran a hand through his hair and tried out his most charming smile on her. "She's a friend of mine. I didn't want you to get the wrong impression."

"No, I'm fairly certain I have the right impression." Jane stood up and placed her tote bag over her shoulder, keeping it close. "Tell me, how many have there been over the years?"

"You have it all wrong," Devon insisted. "You are my wife. I love you."

His words felt like a pit in her stomach. How many times had she longed for them? Begged for them, even. For the slightest sign of affection? Of love? She shook her head. She knew the truth now. Those words would never mean anything to him. "No. You don't."

"Jane," Devon reasoned, although she could see the sweat beads forming on his forehead. "You're being irrational. I've done nothing but love you and take care of you." He held his hands out. "Look around you. Look at the lifestyle I've provided you."

"The lifestyle you provided me?" Jane asked incredulously. It was one thing to pretend to all of their friends, but there were only two people in the room. "You could never afford this on your own. I gave you the lifestyle. And I'm going to take it all back."

Devon's gaze narrowed. He took a step forward, and Jane moved out of his reach. "What are you talking about?"

His voice sounded murderous, and Jane felt her knees go weak. Her plan had sounded so simple and been so easy, but telling him… She hadn't thought about what telling him would be like. She had hoped to somehow just slip away and put all of this behind her. But, of course, that would never be the case.

Be strong, my love.

Her mother's voice resonated through her head. Steeling herself, Jane rushed through the speech she had practiced so many times over the past several weeks. She barely heard the words come out of her own mouth–she just repeated them in a crazed rush. "I've frozen all of our assets. All of MY money will be transferred into a trust in my name only. You are free to keep your earnings. You can have the condo and your car as well. The rest will be divided up…"

"What are you talking about?" Devon repeated, regarding her as if she'd lost her mind. His words were like a slap, bringing her back to reality.

"I'm talking about our divorce, Devon," she replied, sticking to her story. She couldn't let herself slip now.

Devon seemed to freeze in time and, in an instant, reinvent himself. His body went limp, and he slumped forward, placing his hands on his thighs. Jane gripped her bag close to her chest, unsure of what to make of this sudden change in demeanor. When, he stood up again, all of the anger had magically disappeared from his face, and he looked shocked by her words.

"Divorce?" Devon appeared truly stunned to hear

the words come from her mouth. "We're not getting a divorce, Jane." He smiled at her, talking to her as if she were a small child. She thought he probably didn't believe she had really moved the money – she would never have attempted something so bold. She also suspected he didn't take her threats seriously. After all, leaving him would take a tremendous amount of resolve. "We committed to each other – for better or worse, remember?"

She remembered. She remembered the rest of the vows just as well.

Until death do us part...

"You don't love me, Devon," she stated. "Why do you want to pretend?"

"Yes, I do." Devon dropped to his knees dramatically before her, saying passionately, "I love you, and I want to have babies with you."

She didn't believe him, but still, Jane squeezed her eyes closed and stepped around him. "Don't say that." It was the one thing she had held out hope for. The card he always held over her head. She had wanted a baby so badly. Had been so certain that a baby would make their lives stronger. Would give her the love and affection she so strongly desired. Would make them a family. And every time...every single time...Devon would yank that rug out from under her. He practically forced her birth control pills down her throat every day. A baby would be an intrusion on their life. Would ruin the perfection they, no, he, had created.

But, at this moment, Devon seemed overcome with the idea, as if it were something he had just thought of. "Of course. We should have a baby."

Jane felt her heart squeezing inside her chest,

threatening to burst from inside her.

Devon stood up and began pacing the room, talking as if to himself. "Why didn't I think of this before? Your father told me you were the best thing that ever happened to him. You were the perfect substitute after his wife passed away."

Jane felt the tears slide down her face. She couldn't help it. Her heart was breaking inside of her.

She could hear the manic excitement in Devon's voice. "We'll have a little girl, of course."

He clapped his hands together and continued walking across the room. His back was to her, but she could see the bounce in his step. He was regaining confidence with every new thought.

Jane pulled her tote bag from her shoulder. She felt trapped, cornered like a caged animal. How did things end up this way? She just wanted a divorce. She wanted out. She didn't want to talk about babies…

Devon caressed the side of the bed. His expression was a twisted mixture of maniacal pleasure. "She'll grow up to be just like you."

Jane's composure broke. Dropping her bag, she yelled, "Shut up."

Devon turned at the sound of her voice. He had a triumphant smile on his face, which slid as soon as he saw her.

She leveled the pistol she held in her hands toward his chest.

"What do you think you are doing?" His voice sounded incredulous as he stared at her in shock.

"I'm protecting myself," Jane said calmly, even though her insides felt like they were spiraling out of control. She had been passive all of her life. She had never made waves, never asked questions. At this moment, she felt as if she were fighting for her very life. She was petrified.

"You are being ridiculous," he said, attempting to take a step toward her.

He stopped just out of her reach. Jane felt her knees weaken and thought her heart would beat out of her chest, but she said with a resolve she hadn't known she possessed, "I would never let you bring another life into this world. You're just like my father."

"Your father loved you."

Jane shook her head vehemently. "No, he didn't. He didn't love either me or my mother. He killed my mother as surely as if he had stood over her and pulled the trigger himself. Then he treated me like a servant for years before selling me to you. So you could do the same thing." She spit out the words. "Well, I'll be damned if I let you do that to anyone else."

Jane held the gun firm. All she had to do was pull the trigger and the nightmare would be over. Her finger tightened on the device. She felt the power of the small instrument in her hand.

All she had to do was pull the trigger.

And the nightmare would be over.

She stood paralyzed.

All she had to do was pull the trigger.

Devon regarded her for a long moment as if inspecting a foreign specimen that had landed on the floor in front of him. And then, slowly and deliberately, he began to clap. "Bravo, Jane. Well done. I had no idea you were such a great actress. Only one small criticism."

Taken aback, Jane moved her eyes from his chest to his face. What was he talking about? And why was he smiling like that?

In that instant, he lunged forward and grabbed the gun from her hand. He was infinitely stronger than her, and she yelped as he yanked her head back by her hair and placed the gun to her jaw. His voice was low and menacing as he whispered in her ear. "You should have pulled the trigger."

Jane felt her insides melt as she realized the gravity of her situation. She had been crazy to think she could ever overpower her husband. Not only was he much stronger than she; he was insane. Now, she was going to pay for her hesitation. Most likely with her life.

With the coldness of the gunmetal against her jaw, Jane remained still. She spoke through clenched teeth. "Are you going to kill me now?"

"Now?" Devon laughed.

He threw the gun across the room and with a savage pull of her hair spun her around to face him. She felt the strands of hair being pulled from their roots.

"That would be too easy." He held her face so close to his that the spittle from his mouth hit her lips.

Still holding her firmly by the hair with one hand, he stroked the other hand down the side of her cheek. She flinched, but was unable to move without sending shooting pain down her skull. He smiled, and his eyes danced with malice. "No, Jane, I'm not going to kill you. I'm going to teach you."

With a vicious yank, he threw her down on the bed. She landed on her bottom. Keeping her feet flat on the bed, knees raised, she placed her hands behind her and scrambled into a seated position. If he managed to pin her down, she would be completely helpless. But it seemed Devon wasn't finished making his point. He didn't make a move in her direction. Instead, he stood over her and said with an evil glint in his eye. "I thought I had done so well with you. You were the perfect wife – subservient, obedient, and completely submissive." He clenched his jaw in anger. "You had such a good thing – why did you go and have to ruin it?"

As he rubbed his chin in contemplation, Jane took the opportunity to scoot farther away from him on the bed. The gun lay on the floor next to the bed. If she could put enough distance, maybe she could make a grab for it.

Devon stood at the end of the bed, staring at her. "I have to admit – I was getting a little bored with you. You made things so easy, probably too easy." He nodded, as if to himself. "Yes, I am going to enjoy breaking you down." He smiled. "This time, I'll make sure you never run."

She scooted again, and this time he noticed. He grabbed her arm and pulled her viciously toward him. He held her right up against his face and said in a low, dangerous voice. "If you thought any of your lessons so far had been rough, that is nothing compared to what I'm going to do to you now."

A wave of nausea crashed through her insides. She didn't doubt his sincerity for a second. Killing her would have been a blessing. He was going to hurt her in ways she couldn't even imagine. She went limp in his arms, searching internally for her safe place. She wouldn't be able to bear the brutality of his attack in the present. She would have to escape somewhere far away and then deal with the consequences later. It was the only way she could survive.

No baby, don't leave. You have to stay in the present. You have to escape.

"Mama?" Jane lifted her head and looked around. All she saw was a pair of dark, glittering eyes.

"Nope. Your mama's not here, my darling. Only me," Devon caressed her cheek and then, in a split second, pulled his hand back and slapped her. Hard. Her head swam and red dots danced in front of her eyes as her head snapped back under the force of his hand. Devon put his hands in her hair and lifted her head so that she faced him. She barely had time to recover her focus when he hit her again, this time with his hand closed into a fist. He connected with the corner of her eye, and she felt an explosion of pain behind her eye socket. She wanted to collapse from the pain, but Devon held her upright.

With his hand still wrapped in her hair, Devon caressed her cheek again. "Oh, my–I think that's going to leave a bruise." He laughed and touched her eye. "You know how much I hate to mark up that pretty face of yours."

He lay her down on the bed. She didn't have the will to move as he stepped back and removed his belt. "But don't you worry–there is plenty of other damage that I can inflict." His laugh grew malicious. "I have all sorts of ideas."

Jane groaned. Her face felt burning hot, and her eye throbbed. And she knew that was nothing compared to the pain she would be forced to endure. She wanted to curl up into a ball and disappear until everything was over. Yes, she thought dreamily, she just wanted to disappear.

No, Jane. Don't leave. You have to run. Now.

Jane opened her eyes. The one was swollen, and she could barely see out of it, but she noticed Devon had moved to the nightstand and was removing his clothes. He clearly assumed that she had stopped fighting. It was a safe assumption. She had always succumbed before.

But this time, she had an angel looking after her.

Run, Jane. Now.

Devon turned his back to her and began removing his shirt. Jane mustered every ounce of energy she possessed and scrambled off the bed and took off for the door. The gun was too close to where Devon was standing, and she would never be able to reach it and then aim it before he got it away from her. Her only chance of survival was to get out of the house.

"Bitch," Devon shouted and took off after her. He reached for her as she scurried across the room. Luckily for her, his hands were still entangled inside the long sleeves of his dress shirt, and he couldn't grab hold of her.

She slithered through his grasp and sprinted out the bedroom door. Devon ripped off his shirt, throwing it to the ground, and took off after her, screaming, "This time I will kill you, you bitch."

As she reached the landing of the staircase, he reached her and grabbed for her leg. She screamed and pulled out of his grip. He wrapped his hands around her ankle, working to pull her down, but he was off balance, and she managed to free her leg. She stood at the top of the stairway, her world spinning uncontrollably around her, staring back at Devon. With a growl of anger, he lunged for her, throwing his body at her. At the last split second, she stepped out of the way and Devon toppled down the top step. He was completely off balance and unable to regain his footing. His movements appeared to be in slow motion as he waved his hands in the air trying to balance himself. The floating staircase, Devon's masterpiece of art, had no rails to support him.

"Jane," he shouted as he worked desperately to right himself. His face grew into a mask of shock as he tilted sideways with nothing to hold onto. "Help me."

The words reached Jane's ears as if through a tunnel. Her head was swimming in a fog of pain and numbness.

The fall to the first floor took an eternity as Devon's hands waved in the air and then finally stiffened as he tried to break his fall. The crunch of bones breaking echoed up the stairs as he hit the solid concrete floor.

After that, there was silence.

Jane watched the fall unmoving from the top of the stairs. Only a matter of seconds had passed since she first moved from the bed, but in that instant, her life had changed forever.

Jane leaned forward slightly to look over the staircase to the floor below.

Her heart stopped beating for a second at the sight below her. She had imagined a thousand different scenarios of how things would end, but this had not been one of them.

It was clear from the angle at which Devon lay that he had broken his neck in the fall.

She knew there would be tears to shed and condolences to accept, but for this one pure second, Jane allowed herself to be free. It was over. Really, truly over.

Tears rolled down her face, but not for Devon.

"Mama," she said aloud. "Thank you for saving me." The tears came down a little harder. "I miss you so much. I'm so sorry for what you went through. I wish I could have helped you."

I love you, baby. And I promise–I will always be

239

here for you.

Jane wiped away the tears, turned, and went back into the bedroom. Using the landline in her bedroom, she dialed 9-1-1.

"9-1-1. What is your emergency?"

Jane touched her eye, which felt swollen and tender, and looked around the room which showed clear signs of a struggle. She knew she would not have to answer many questions about what happened. She cleared her throat and said, "There's been an accident. My husband is dead."

The operator took her information, and within minutes, she could hear sirens wailing in the distance.

As she waited for help to arrive, she looked down at the small cell phone in her hand. This one simple device had started the sequence of events leading to this very moment. After tonight, she would never need to use it again.

For the last time, she pushed the green call button, hitting reply to the last message received, and typed in the words:

IT'S OVER. WE'RE FREE.

www.ingramcontent.com/pod-product-compliance
Lightning Source LLC
Chambersburg PA
CBHW070107030726
47506CB00002B/633